A WITCHY BUSINESS

HARPER GRANT MYSTERY SERIES BOOK ONE

DANICA BRITTON

For Chris

CHAPTER 1

"If he were my son, I would tell him to pull up his britches and stop making such a fuss."

I looked up and paused in my wiping down of table fifteen. I was working the morning shift in Archie's Diner and had been run off my feet all morning.

"No one says britches these days, Loretta," I said, and then followed her gaze to look at the young boy she'd been referring to.

Tommy Breton was six years old and a bundle of trouble. His mother was tapping something out on her cell phone, completely ignoring Tommy as he whined about wanting another donut and smeared his jelly-covered face all over the window pane I had cleaned earlier that morning.

"And just look at the state of that table! Honestly, I hate to think what their home looks like." Loretta pursed her lips in a firm line.

I had to agree with her. As Tommy and his mother got up from their seats, the devastation they'd left behind was clear to see. The table was covered with bits of food, and the floor hadn't escaped unscathed either.

I squirted the top of the table with cleaning solution and quickly wiped away the crumbs and sticky fingermarks that Tommy had left behind.

Loretta peered over my shoulder, inspecting the damage.

I walked across the diner to get the broom. Fortunately, we still had a little while before the lunchtime rush hit, so I had a chance to clear up after Tommy.

He and his mother came in for breakfast nearly every day. I couldn't say I blamed her. She must've enjoyed the rest from cleaning up after him.

"Well, aren't you going to say something?" Loretta asked sharply as I began to sweep under the table.

Tommy and his mother were now outside. His mother was still engrossed with her cell phone, and Tommy had now started hammering on the outside of the glass window. He really was full of mischief.

I didn't want to say anything to upset Archie's customers, though. I had enough trouble fitting in around here as it was, and I didn't want to give anyone more reasons to treat me like an outsider.

I opened my mouth to reply to Loretta but closed it again quickly when I heard Archie's footsteps as he walked towards us.

"How are we getting on out here?" Archie asked cheerfully.

The smile dropped from his face as he looked in disapproval at the state of the floor.

"Almost finished here," I said as I swept around his feet.

Archie waved his hand at Tommy, trying to get him to stop pounding on the window. His mother was still standing next to him, tapping away on her cell phone.

"Honestly, that child is impossible," Archie grumbled under his breath.

Archie is my boss, and the diner is named after him. I had been working there for five years, and the job was a pretty good one. Archie was a sweet guy and an easygoing boss. He was only a couple of years older than me, but from the way he acted sometimes, you might guess he was nearer my Grandma's age.

As Grandma Grant would say, Archie was definitely set in his ways.

Of course, he wasn't quite as set in his ways as Loretta.

I finished sweeping up the mess under the table and put the broom back in the closet just as the first patrons started arriving for lunch.

Archie wandered over to greet them, and when he was just

out of earshot, I turned around to find Loretta directly behind me.

"I think Archie's sweet on you," Loretta said.

"Don't be ridiculous," I muttered, hoping that Archie and the new arrivals wouldn't notice.

I hoped he wasn't sweet on me. Archie wasn't my type, but he was a nice guy, and I wouldn't want to hurt him.

I wasn't looking for a relationship. It isn't easy to form connections with people when you live the kind of life I do.

I don't want to make you think I'm a freak. Most of the time, I'm pretty normal. In fact, until my sixteenth birthday, I was the textbook example of a normal girl.

I was an A-grade student most of the time, except when it came to Math. I've always hated Math.

I grew up with my parents in New York City, along with my two sisters, Jess and Lily. My father was a bank manager, and my mother was an elementary school teacher. We holidayed in Cape Cod every year and lived comfortably. I had a happy, secure childhood.

Things didn't turn weird until after my sixteenth birthday.

Until then, we were pretty much the poster family for typical, ordinary American life. I can't emphasize that enough. We were one hundred percent average. That's why it made what happened next so much harder to deal with.

When I turned sixteen, slightly odd things started happening to me.

It wasn't an easy thing to cope with, especially as my mother and father seemed determined to ignore it. They thought if they brushed it under the carpet and carried on as normal, the problem would go away.

It wasn't until my Grandma came to visit us that summer, I finally understood what was happening to me. She explained things to me in a way that made sense.

Okay, so I didn't exactly take it well when she first told me. I mean, how would you take it if someone told you you were a witch?

But that's what Grandma Grant had told me. She sat me down one evening at the scrubbed pine table, in the kitchen of my parent's New York home, and as she handed me a mug of her special cocoa, she told me why these strange things had been happening.

I was very surprised to learn that I, Harper Grant, was one of a long line of witches. I'd been assuming there was something seriously wrong with me — maybe some medical problem was causing me to hallucinate, or I was just plain losing my mind, but witchcraft? That hadn't been a possibility I'd considered.

Grandma Grant told me the Grant family of witches were part of an ancient coven. As our witch powers were hereditary, she'd been waiting for me to show the signs.

But there was something that didn't seem to make sense: My parents were Mr. and Mrs. Normal.

Grandma Grant explained that away by saying sometimes the

magic could skip a generation, and it seemed that my father had never shown any magical abilities at all.

My parents were very agitated every time I brought the subject up. They'd hoped all three of their girls would be just as normal as they were, and they had a hard time accepting that I was different.

As the oldest girl, I was the first one to experience the changes, but a year later, my sister Jess went through a very similar transformation.

It was tough going, that first couple of years. With our parents deliberately avoiding any conversations about our abilities, we felt awkward and alone.

It's not easy to go through something like that and not be able to talk about it, so we ended up moving down here to live with Grandma Grant in the small town of Abbott Cove.

That had been five years ago. Archie had given me a job at the diner, and I hadn't looked back.

I sometimes missed the anonymity of city life, but I loved the atmosphere of the small town, although I wasn't so keen on the gossiping and everybody knowing each other's business.

"Earth to Harper," Loretta said hovering beside me.

Loretta nodded at the table.

I'd been refilling the salt containers, and I'd let them overflow. I cursed under my breath and grabbed a cloth. I'd been feeling distracted today. Almost as if I was expecting something major to happen, but so far today had been a typical one with nothing exciting or out of the usual occurring at all.

I sometimes thought my distraction was all part of my powers, perhaps a sign something was about to happen, but Grandma Grant said it wasn't a power. She told me I was just scatter-brained. She could be a little blunt at times.

But despite what Grandma Grant said, when I felt out of sorts and distracted like this, it usually meant something important was about to happen.

Most of the time I kept the feeling under control, but for some reason, today, I felt very nervous.

"Archie is talking to you," Loretta said, and I looked over to the corner of the diner, and saw she was right.

Archie was looking at me with his eyebrows raised expectantly.

I quickly finished tidying up the mess I'd made, and then walked over. Archie was talking to Chief Wickham, our chief of police, who was fast approaching retirement age.

"Hi, Harper," the chief said with a broad smile. He was a good man and had always been kind to me, my sister and my Grandma.

Sometimes, I got the feeling he suspected that we might be a little different from other families, but he had never said anything or asked any awkward questions.

"Hello, Chief Wickham. What can I get you? Your usual?"

"Aha, I'm getting predictable," Chief Wickham said. He

always had the clam chowder when he stopped for lunch at the diner.

"I don't blame you, Chief," Archie said. "Sarah makes the finest clam chowder in the county." He turned to me. "Why don't you take your break after you've given Sarah the order, Harper? I'll hold the fort until you get back."

I smiled and thanked him and took the order through into the kitchen to give to Sarah, the cook.

"Let me guess," Sarah said as I walked into the kitchen. "The chief is having clam chowder?"

I grinned at Sarah. "Right first time," I said, pinning the order to the board. "I'm heading out to lunch now. I'm going to pop over to the library to see Jess, but I won't be long."

Sarah pointed at the counter next to me. "I've prepared your lunch over there. There's a container of leek and potato soup, some crusty rolls and a couple of slices of cherry pie."

I gave Sarah a broad smile. "Thanks. You're an angel."

There were definite benefits to working at the diner, and getting to sample Sarah's cooking for free was high on the list.

"What have you got there?" Loretta asked me, peering into the basket over my arm just before I left the diner.

"Lunch," I whispered. "Leek and potato soup and cherry pie."

Loretta's eyes widened slightly, and her face took on a dreamy look. "Cherry pie. That used to be my favorite. What I wouldn't give for a slice of that right now."

I bowed my head as I spoke to Loretta, and used my hand to cover my mouth. It wouldn't do for Archie or Chief Wickham to see me apparently talking to myself. The town thought I was kooky enough as it was.

"I think that's the worst thing about being a ghost. Life without dessert," Loretta said and then floated off back through the wall towards the kitchen.

CHAPTER 2

I WATCHED Loretta float off and then headed out of the diner, turning down Main Street.

The seagulls were squawking out in the harbor as old man Jackson had just brought in his fishing boat.

He called out, and I waved back, hurrying along the street towards the town library where my sister Jess worked.

Abbott Cove is on the coast of Maine. It's a small dot on the map, and you can walk through the entire town in fifteen minutes. But despite its size, it feels like home to me now, and I've grown to love it.

There's not much to do in town, though. There's Archie's Diner, of course, a seafood restaurant and a bar near the harbor, and on Main Street, there is a grocery shop along with a couple of smaller shops, selling things like fridge magnets and decorative mugs — the usual tourist stuff.

About twice a week, we get a busload of tourists visiting, and they stroll about the town, eating ice creams and buying knickknacks.

On those days, the diner is fit to burst, and I don't get to take breaks any longer than five minutes at a time, but I can't complain as it pays my wages.

Jess was sorting through some books from Mrs. Lyttleton as I entered the library, and scanning the barcodes to return them to the system.

My sister is perfectly suited to working in the library. She'd always had her nose buried in a book as a child, and was never happier than when she was surrounded by storybooks.

When she was finished, I waved the cherry pie under her nose.

"Oh, yum, Sarah's cherry pie. It's my favorite."

Jess lifted the lid off the carton of soup and breathed in the steamy vapor. "The soup smells amazing, too. I'm starving. Did I tell you how much I like you working at the diner?"

"You say that every single time I bring you a sample of Sarah's cooking."

As it was only Jess who manned the library front desk, when we took our lunch through to the staff area at the back, Jess sat near the doorway, so she could see if anyone came in and needed assistance.

The soup was still hot, so I poured it into bowls and added a little black pepper to mine, and we both dug in.

"Do you think you'll be home for dinner tonight?" Jess asked. "We're supposed to be eating dinner at Grandma's."

I nodded, and between sips of hot soup, I said, "Yes, I'll be there. I'm not working late tonight."

Grandma Grant lived in the ancestral Grant family home, a huge house at the edge of town, set on a large plot of land where she grew a variety of plants and ran a small nursery business.

Jess and I tended to eat there at least twice a week, and it was a nice way to spend time with each other without actually living in the same house as Grandma.

I love my Grandma dearly, but she can be a little odd at times.

I live with Jess in a small cottage about a minutes' walk from Grandma's house. It has three bedrooms, a large kitchen-diner, and a cozy lounge. It's the perfect size for us.

Grandma, on the other hand, rattled around the large ancestral house, but she liked it that way. My grandfather had died forty years ago, and she'd lived alone ever since and was very set in her ways.

"Good," Jess said, putting her empty bowl on the counter. "Because I think you should talk to her."

I frowned. "Who?"

"Grandma, of course," Jess said impatiently. "I think she's up to something. I saw her this morning, and she was acting very strangely."

"How is that any different from usual?"

"I'm telling you she's up to something. She was ever so secretive."

Uh oh. That didn't sound good. The last time Grandma Grant had been up to something, she cast a spell on Old Captain Bryant's car. He'd cut her off at the lights, and Grandma had cast a spell that made his car bunny hop all the way home.

Of course, no one could prove that it was actually her, but Jess and I knew.

"I've got a new book," Jess said as she put both our bowls in the sink and started washing up.

She pointed towards the counter, and I saw a large red and gold, leather-bound book, wrapped in white tissue paper.

I stood up and took a closer look. The writing on the front looked like old English.

"It's a book of spells," Jess said, her eyes gleaming with excitement.

I smiled at her enthusiasm, but I didn't share it. Jess was a traditional witch, like Grandma Grant. She was quite brilliant at spells and especially skilled in protection spells.

I'd never been very good at them. I'd always found it a bit like studying. A pinch of this and a sprinkle of that, and then having to say all the words in the right order. It really wasn't for me. That wasn't where my abilities lay.

I had a different talent.

My witchy ability was being able to see ghosts like Loretta.

It was quite disconcerting at first. The first time it happened had been just after my sixteenth birthday. I'd been to the theater with a friend, and we'd just left the cinema and rounded the corner when we saw a group of people gathered on the road and heard approaching sirens.

We were jostled forward, closer to the crowd, and that's when I saw the old lady lying on the floor.

She'd been hit by a car, and it looked pretty bad. My friend covered her eyes, and I'd wanted to do the same, but something made me keep looking. To my astonishment, I saw the ghost of the little old lady float upward, look down at her prone body on the floor and give a little shrug.

I stared as she spun in a circle and spiraled upwards into the sky until she disappeared.

I blinked a couple of times and put the vision down to the fact I'd just watched a horror movie, but that incident had turned out to be the first of many.

I kept quiet about it at first. I mean you don't want people to think you're going crazy, do you? And how exactly do you explain a vision like that to someone?

But Grandma Grant had known. She arrived in New York just a couple of weeks after my sixteenth birthday.

She'd waited until we were alone in the kitchen one evening after dinner, and then asked me whether I'd noticed anything strange lately.

Of course, that could have meant anything. So I hedged

around the subject for a bit, not wanting to tell her I had been hallucinating.

After a while, she got tired of it and said bluntly. "Harper Grant, stop giving me the runaround. Are you a witch, or not?"

Naturally, when she found out that I could see ghosts she was very pleased. I was glad someone was. At that point, I would have given anything to go back to being boring old Harper.

Apparently, we hadn't had one of my type of witch, a ghost-seer, in the family for generations. She'd told me she had hopes for her brother once, but unfortunately, his hallucinations had turned out to be a result of his drinking problem rather than any magical ability.

"It's the town festival tomorrow. Do you think Grandma is up to something?" Jess asked. "I bet she's got something planned."

Grandma didn't think it was important to keep the fact that we were witches a secret. She didn't broadcast it, but she didn't exactly keep it quiet either. Jess and I would prefer people didn't know. Life could be hard enough as a witch, without your neighbors gossiping about you.

"I'd forgotten about the festival. I hope she isn't planning anything. She hasn't even mentioned going, so maybe she's forgotten about it."

Jess raised an eyebrow. "Unlikely. She never forgets anything. She's got a memory like an elephant. Anyway, I have to go. Elizabeth Naggington is making me do tarot readings. Can you believe it? She knows it makes me uncomfortable, but that woman doesn't take no for an answer."

Elizabeth Naggington was one of the town's most notorious gossips. Bossy and self-righteous, she didn't have many friends in Abbott Cove. She had a brow-beaten husband and son, but most other people, including me, did their best to avoid her.

I nodded as I dished up the cherry pie. Jessica was right Elizabeth Naggington was awful. Luckily so far, I'd managed to avoid being roped into helping with one of the stalls.

"Maybe whatever Grandma Grant is planning involves the festival," Jess suggested.

"I almost hope it does. Then we could call the whole thing off. Elizabeth does have a habit of taking control of everything and making everyone miserable."

I know. I'm a terrible person with no community spirit, but seriously? Town gatherings weren't any fun when you tried to plan them with military precision as Elizabeth Naggington did.

Bossing everyone about was just asking for trouble.

CHAPTER 3

LUNCH WAS ALWAYS our busiest time, so I didn't stay long with Jess. I got back to the diner just as Chief Wickham was leaving. I held the door open for two customers, coming in just behind me, and when I saw who they were, I felt my shoulders slump.

Loretta made a tutting sound behind me. "Oh no," she said. "Not her again."

It was Elizabeth Naggington and husband Robert. Nothing was ever good enough for Elizabeth. She was one of those people who found fault with everything.

Last time she'd visited the diner, she complained that the windows were letting in too much sun. On another occasion, she moaned that the salt had come out too fast and ruined her meal. She'd been visiting the diner for years, and the salt shakers were exactly the same as they'd always been.

Her poor beleaguered husband, Robert, followed her around

with a morose expression on his face. Occasionally, he would look up apologetically, blink a couple of times and then return his gaze to the floor. It seemed he knew better than to contradict his wife.

Archie must have heard me groan as she walked in.

"Now, now," Archie said. "The customer is always right." He gave me a beaming smile, displaying his dimples.

Elizabeth Naggington was a customer who certainly always thought she was right.

"It's all right for you," I whispered to Archie. "You don't have to serve her and listen to her moaning."

"You're overreacting," Archie told me. "She just likes things a certain way. Let me deal with her."

I shrugged. "My pleasure. Go right ahead."

As far as I was concerned, the less time I spent talking to her the better. Plus, if I wasn't serving her, there was less chance of her collaring me to work on one of the stalls for the town festival.

Archie picked up a menu, folded a tea towel over his arm, so he looked like a waiter from a French restaurant and sauntered over to the table.

Elizabeth was already screwing up her nose as she brushed her seat free from imaginary crumbs.

"Look at Lady Muck over there, looking down her nose at everyone and everything," Loretta said from behind me.

Despite my best intentions, I couldn't help but smile. Loretta had hit the nail on the head. Lady Muck described Elizabeth Naggington perfectly.

"Isn't it a glorious day?" Archie was saying to Elizabeth and Robert.

Elizabeth sat down, and her gaze flickered to the window. "The heat plays havoc with my complexion. I prefer the weather when it's cloudy. It's completely the wrong sort of weather for this time of year."

Elizabeth's mouth turned down at the corners, and she glared at the cloudless sky.

I rolled my eyes. It was a beautiful day. The leaves were just beginning to turn, and the yellow and red leaves set against the vivid blue of the sky made a very attractive sight. Days like today were exactly the reason we had so many tourists visiting our small town of Abbott Cove.

Surely Archie would now have to give up and admit that Elizabeth would never be happy with anything.

But Archie soldiered on, determined to win her over.

"The soup of the day is leek and potato," he said. "I like all of Sarah's soups, but the leek and potato is really something special."

"I just hope the potatoes aren't too old, like they were last time," Elizabeth sniped.

That just wasn't true. Sarah who worked in the kitchen was a fabulous cook and her leek and potato soup was to die for. Archie made sure to buy the best quality ingredients, too.

Archie looked a little taken aback, but he carried on bravely. "We have a fillet of beef that's—"

"I wouldn't dream of having fillet of beef here," Elizabeth said rudely. "Not in a provincial diner like this."

Archie's face turned a bright red as he stared down at her furiously.

"I'll just let you look through the menu then," he said through gritted teeth, dropping the menu on the table. "Harper will be over to take your order soon."

He stalked off, and as he passed me, he said, "That woman is simply intolerable."

I could have told him that.

I gave Elizabeth and Robert a couple more minutes to look at the menu, even though it hadn't changed much since their last visit. For someone who looks down her nose at the cooking, Elizabeth visited the diner an awful lot.

"Hello," I said brightly, smiling at Robert and Elizabeth as I walked up to their table to take their order.

"Hello, Harper," Robert said and gave me a half-hearted smile.

Elizabeth looked at me suspiciously. "I'll have the shrimp sandwich," she said. "And Robert will have the chicken salad. We'll share a pitcher of iced tea."

"Right," I said cheerfully, and wrote it down on my order pad.

"Actually, dear, I thought I might try the beef today," Robert said tentatively.

"Don't be ridiculous, Robert. You know red meat doesn't agree with your digestion." She looked at me pointedly. "He'll have the chicken salad."

She glared at me as if she was waiting for me to contradict her, but I didn't dare.

I hesitated by their table for a moment, but it didn't seem as if Robert was going to argue the point with his wife either, so I poured them both some water and headed to the kitchen to give Sarah the order.

The lunch rush was particularly busy, as a busload of tourists arrived out of the blue. We were usually forewarned so Archie could hire an extra pair of hands, but now and again we had a surprise arrival.

Archie pitched in to help me, but we were both rushed off our feet.

Elizabeth didn't appreciate waiting.

As the Naggingtons had ordered before we were inundated by the new arrivals, I'd managed to get their salad and sandwich out quickly, but I wasn't quick enough topping up their drinks for Elizabeth's liking.

I had just gone back for the new pitcher of iced tea when I heard a large bang as Elizabeth slapped her palm on the table.

"This is simply unforgivable," she said in a high-pitched voice.

Several heads swiveled around to see who was making a fuss.

"It's a disgrace," Elizabeth continued. "And this is absolutely the last time I eat in this awful little diner."

She stood up and picked up her purse, tucking it under her arm. "Come along, Robert. We are leaving."

Robert, who had been just about to take a mouthful of chicken, paused with the fork halfway to his mouth. "But, dear, I haven't finished…"

Elizabeth gave him such a look that I thought he might burst into flames on the spot.

"We are regulars," Elizabeth said. "And these tourists are being served before us. No, Robert, I will not stand to be treated this way, and neither will you. Now, get up. We're leaving."

Robert quickly put down his fork and walked around the table to offer his wife his arm so he could escort her out of the diner.

I glanced at Archie and could see that his cheeks were bright red again, and he was trembling with rage.

Just before they reached the door, Elizabeth turned around and looked past me to the kitchen hatch, where Sarah stood, peering out to see what all the noise was about.

"And you can tell the cook that was quite simply the worst shrimp I have ever eaten."

The entire diner was now focused on Elizabeth Naggington as she flounced out.

I heard Sarah mutter a curse behind me. "Someone needs to do something about that woman."

The rest of the lunch period passed without too much fuss. I enjoyed being busy. I found that the time flew around, and I enjoyed having the tourists visit. It was nice to see new faces, and it was important for Abbott Cove's economy to get tourists.

I was feeling a little guilty, though. I knew it was my fault. I'd been too slow with the second pitcher of iced tea, and that had caused Elizabeth to go off the deep end.

After the last of the tourists had left, cheerfully waving good-bye, I apologized to Archie.

"I'm sorry. I should have gotten them refills faster."

"Nonsense," he said. "Their glasses weren't even empty. She just wanted something to complain about, she's just a nasty, old…"

My eyes widened. I'd never seen Archie so angry. He was normally very easy-going.

He shook his head. "Anyway, let's forget about all that unpleasantness. Things should hopefully quieten down a little now."

CHAPTER 4

THE AFTERNOON at the diner passed without any more calamities. There weren't many customers, and we were glad of the chance to get our breath back after such a busy lunch. An hour before my shift was due to end, Archie told me to leave early, and he would finish up.

Sarah gave me three large slices of her delicious carrot cake to take home as she knew I was having dinner with Grandma Grant and Jess.

I called goodbye to Archie and stepped outside the diner, not looking where I was going, and as I stepped forward, I collided with a wall of hard muscle.

My gaze traveled upwards, skimming over a broad chest, muscular shoulders, and a strong jaw and focused on the most sparkling blue eyes I'd ever seen.

I have to admit I gaped a little as I drank in the tall, dark, handsome figure in front of me.

He looked like he had just stepped off the cover of a magazine. His tanned skin, piercing blue eyes and strong jaw were a dangerous combination. He was dressed in a pair of jeans and a smart shirt that hugged his broad shoulders. They may have been casual clothes, but somehow on him, the effect was sharp yet formal. The only relaxed thing about him was his dark hair, which tumbled forward over his forehead.

He raked his fingers through his hair and stared down at me, raising an eyebrow.

"Whoa. Watch where you're going there, Harper," said a familiar voice, and for the first time, I realized that I wasn't alone with this handsome stranger. Chief Wickham stood next to him.

Flustered, I took a quick step backward. "Sorry. My mistake. I was in a rush."

"No harm done," the handsome stranger said, his mouth twitching with a smile as he noticed the effect he had on me.

For some reason, I found that irritating.

I tried to act as if I wasn't bothered by his presence in the slightest. I opened the cardboard carton and checked on my carrot cake, which thankfully had escaped the collision without getting squished.

"Harper, I'd like to introduce you to my new deputy, Joe McGrady," Chief Wickham said.

"It's a pleasure to meet you." Joe held out his hand.

When I placed my hand in his warm one, I felt a tingle run along the length of my arm.

I wasn't sure whether that was simply my reaction to a good-looking guy -- I was female after all -- or whether it was something magical in the air... Maybe a warning.

I'd been feeling out of sorts all day. Almost as if the universe was warning me something big was about to happen.

I quickly removed my hand and smiled at him and Chief Wickham.

"So, you've just moved to town," I said.

Way to go, Harper. Bowl him over with your incredible ability to point out the obvious.

"Yes, I've just moved here from New York City."

I frowned. "I imagine that's quite a change. I'm sure you'll find our little town quite boring in comparison."

"Boring sounds good to me after what I've been through. I'm after peace and quiet, and this town appeals to me on all levels."

Immediately, I was intrigued. What had he been through?

"Well, isn't he a very good-looking young man," Loretta said as she hovered behind me.

Loretta chose the worst moments to appear. She didn't usually stray far from the diner, which was where she felt safe, but obviously, Joe McGrady's appearance had attracted her attention.

I did my best to ignore her and just grinned like a crazy person at Chief Wickham and Joe McGrady.

"If only I was ten years younger," Loretta swooned.

Try thirty years, I thought snappily. Plus, the small matter that she was a ghost. I turned to glare at Loretta over my shoulder.

The trouble was, I was so focused on not speaking aloud to Loretta, I hadn't noticed that Chief Wickham and Joe were both waiting for me to reply to something they'd just said.

Impressive. That had to be a record even for me. In less than sixty seconds, I'd managed to convince Joe I was an oddball.

I felt my cheeks go warm under his gaze.

Chief Wickham was now looking at us both with a frown on his face. "Right, well, don't let us hold you up, Harper. Say hello to your Grandma and Jess for me. No doubt, I'll see you at the festival tomorrow."

"Yes, I'll be there, Chief. Nice meeting you, Joe."

I quickly walked past them and continued along Main Street. I had a strong feeling I'd managed to make a complete fool of myself. Sometimes, it was hard to act like a normal person, especially with Loretta hovering over my shoulder.

I sighed. There went my chances of impressing the first good-looking man to wander into Abbott Cove for years. Then I looked down at my takeaway carton and shrugged. I still had cake. Every cloud had a silver lining.

* * *

As I WALKED up to Grandma Grant's house, I became aware of a strange rustling noise coming from the greenhouse.

I picked my way through the overgrown path, which led to the large glass doors, and then peered in.

Grandma Grant was right at the back, leaning over a very large plant pot and muttering something to herself.

There was a large, brown, leather-bound book open on the trestle table, covered with flecks of compost.

I frowned. Jess had been right. She was up to something.

"Grandma?"

Grandma Grant straightened up and whirled around with a speed that made me jump.

"What are you doing here? Are you spying on me?"

Grandma Grant's cat, Athena, appeared out of nowhere and wound herself around my legs. As grumpy and cantankerous as Grandma Grant could be with people, she was a pushover when it came to Athena. She was always sneaking the cat little treats when she thought Jess and I weren't looking.

I shifted the box of carrot cake under my arm. "I'm not spying. I'm simply saying hello. You asked us for dinner remember."

Grandma Grant walked towards me briskly, narrowing her eyes and slapping her hands together to rid them of the compost.

"Well, you're early."

"Nice to see you, too. There's nothing like a warm welcome," I muttered as I leaned down to pet Athena. "What were you doing in there anyway?"

Grandma Grant looked up at me shiftily. She was definitely hiding something. "It's a greenhouse. I was growing plants, what do you think I was doing?"

I frowned. That may have sounded reasonable to anyone who didn't actually know Grandma Grant. The fact was, she was always up to something. When she acted defensively like this, it usually meant she was planning something she shouldn't be.

Jess and I both had suspicions that Grandma cast spells on her plants. Her pumpkins won prizes at the festival every year, and people came from miles around to buy plants from the nursery.

"I hope you weren't using spells on the plants," I said, trying to look over her shoulder.

Grandma's face took on a wounded look. "I can't believe you would suggest such a thing."

"You have won best in show for your pumpkins ten years in a row."

"I have a green thumb."

She put her hands on my shoulders and led me away from the greenhouse. "Anyway," she said and nodded at the box I was carrying. "Have you brought cake? I hope you didn't make it."

Charming.

As witches, we were all skilled in some areas, but none of us were very good cooks. Grandma was probably the best out of all of us. At least, she managed not to burn everything.

"It's carrot cake," I said. "Sarah baked it."

"Oh, thank goodness," Grandma said.

She was trying to divert attention by changing the subject. It was the oldest trick in the book, and I hadn't put up with her mischief-making for the past five years without getting to know some of her tricks.

"Don't change the subject. What were you up to in there?"

Grandma turned to me, with her practiced innocent expression. "I'm sure I don't know what you mean. Come on. Since you're here, we'd better get up to the house so I can make a start on dinner."

I may have suspected Grandma of using spells, but I couldn't prove it, I knew better than to push the point and accuse her directly until I had more evidence.

"If you're looking for someone to cast a spell on, I wish you would put one on Elizabeth Naggington to make her less obnoxious. There must be some sort of anti-moaning spell you could use," I complained as we walked up to the house.

"That wouldn't be proper, Harper. You know witches are supposed to use their powers for good, and only in important situations."

"And is growing the best plants really an important use of a spell?"

Grandma Grant gave me a warning look. "I don't know what you're talking about."

In the kitchen, Grandma Grant started mashing potatoes, and I prepared some green beans. We'd almost finished when Jess joined us.

She put the large book of spells down on the kitchen counter, and Grandma Grant seemed very impressed, hurrying over to take a look. I knew I'd lost them both now. Once they started talking spells, they could be at it for hours.

"I guess I'll finish up here then?" I said taking the gravy off the heat and rolling my eyes when they both ignored me.

We sat at the kitchen table to eat dinner. Despite the fact the Grant family home was huge, with a grand old-fashioned dining room, Grandma Grant only used a couple of the rooms regularly.

I served up dinner and listened to them chatter away about some special new spells. Spells are not my thing, and I'd soon lost track of the conversation.

When they finally paused for breath, I tried to change the subject.

"Are you contributing anything to the festival this year Grandma, aside from your pumpkins?"

Grandma looked up and nodded. "I'm running the cotton candy stall this year."

I smirked, imagining Grandma Grant trying to control the sticky, fluffy sticks of sugar.

I thought, all things considered, I'd gotten off very easily. I was obviously not Elizabeth Naggington's favorite person today, and I doubted she would be calling on me to force me to run one of the stalls tomorrow. It looked like I'd escaped that honor.

But Grandma narrowed her eyes and looked at me. "Don't look so smug, Harper. She called in this afternoon to leave you a note. You're looking after the children's bouncy castle tomorrow."

The smile slid from my face. The children's bouncy castle? Ugh, I really hated Elizabeth Naggington.

CHAPTER 5

THE DAY of the festival dawned bright but chilly. Jess and I both layered up, wearing two sweaters each.

We headed for Grandma's so we could walk down together. We only lived ten minutes' walk from the center of town, and the festival was being held on the school playing field.

The field was almost full already when we got there. Everyone seemed reluctant to be there. It was such a shame.

I remembered a few years back, when Elizabeth Naggington wasn't in charge, this was something that people looked forward to — a celebration of the community, but since Elizabeth had gotten involved, a couple of years ago, no one seemed to have fun anymore.

"Seriously, there must be some kind of spell you could use," I muttered to Grandma Grant and Jess as we trudged across the field towards the stalls.

"That's cheating," Grandma Grant said sharply. "Besides, think of all the fun you'll have with all those lovely children. Say, isn't that little Tommy Breton?"

I turned to see a line of children at the bouncy castle, at the front of the queue was the notorious Tommy Breton, the human equivalent of the Tasmanian devil.

I sighed.

Mrs. Townsend, who was manning the bric-a-brac stall waved to us as we passed.

Archie stood in front of the circle of stalls, looking far too cheerful, as he called for customers for his apple bobbing.

He had a sack of apples by his feet and added some more to the water-filled barrel as we walked past. "Roll up, Roll up. Come and chance your luck at the apple bobbing! Spectacular prizes to be won."

I couldn't see any prizes, spectacular or otherwise. I had a feeling Archie was exaggerating.

Unsurprisingly, there weren't too many customers willing to dunk their heads in the cold water this morning.

Standing beside Archie, Sarah, the chef at the diner, looked thoroughly miserable.

"Ready, Sarah?" Archie said cheerfully slapping her on the shoulder.

Sarah nodded apprehensively and stepped up to the barrel.

He'd obviously coerced Sarah into it. It was a bit harsh, since

Archie was Sarah's boss, so she couldn't really say no. Still, I was glad he hadn't roped me into it, and I slipped quietly past them, heading towards the bouncy castle.

I was almost there when I heard a bloodcurdling scream.

I, along with everybody else in the field, turned to see what had happened.

Water was dripping from Sarah's face. Her bangs were plastered to her forehead.

Archie's face was pinched and white, and his eyes were wide.

I began to feel tingles…something was terribly wrong.

I walked back over to them. "What is it?"

"In there…" Archie pointed at the barrel.

I frowned and stepped closer, putting my hands on the edge as I peered down, and then wished I hadn't.

Elizabeth Naggington's face was staring up at me from the depths of the barrel.

CHAPTER 6

"QUIET, people! Quiet. Can I have your attention please?" Chief Wickham stood in the middle of the field and tried to calm everyone down.

He was supposed to be the judge of the pumpkin competition today. He still wore a smiley sticker on his plaid shirt, declaring him a judge.

Grandma Grant was at my side and whispered in my ear. "Do you think he's still going to judge the best pumpkin?"

I shot her a look of disbelief. "I think he's got bigger things on his mind than that."

She widened her eyes and tried to look innocent. "What? I was just asking. I put a lot of effort into growing those pumpkins."

"I'd like everyone to stick around, and either myself or Joe will have a word with everyone," Chief Wickham said, and then he broke off to talk to poor Sarah, who was absolutely distraught.

Jess joined us and said in a low voice, so no one else would hear, "Have you seen the ghost yet?"

I shook my head. I'd been keeping an eye out, but I hadn't seen any sign of Elizabeth's ghost. Of course, she may have already passed over, but usually, I would have spotted something.

"Perhaps she didn't die here," Grandma Grant said, meaningfully. "The killer could have murdered her somewhere else and then dumped her in the barrel."

Jess shivered, and I looked around the crowd suspiciously. Was somebody here really a murderer? It seemed unlikely that Elizabeth could have climbed into the barrel and drowned herself.

"Can I have a word, ladies?" Joe's deep voice rumbled, and we all jumped.

We looked far from innocent as we turned around to face him.

I tried to smile at him brightly so he wouldn't think I was trying to hide anything. Of course, smiling brightly when a dead body had been found a few feet away from me, probably wasn't the best idea if I was trying to avoid raising his suspicions.

He frowned as he looked at the grin plastered on my face.

"Did you know the deceased?" Joe asked.

"Of course we did," Grandma Grant said impatiently. "Everybody knew Elizabeth Naggington."

Joe nodded and wrote a comment in his notepad.

"What time did you get here today?"

"We'd only just arrived," Jess said.

Joe nodded, but he didn't make another note in his book. Instead, he looked straight at me.

His piercing blue eyes were very disconcerting. I had a strong feeling he didn't trust us.

"And did you all arrive together?"

I nodded, and Jess said, "That's right. Harper and I called in for Grandma Grant on the way down."

"Did you see anything suspicious?"

We all shook our heads.

It was then I saw her. Right at the worst possible moment. The ghost of Elizabeth Naggington was hovering over Joe's shoulder.

I gasped, and then tried to cover my reaction with a cough. It didn't work. Joe looked at me as if I'd grown two heads.

I groaned as Elizabeth drifted away. I could hardly make a run for it and chase after her when Joe was in the middle of questioning us.

"I'm sorry, Miss Grant," Joe said to me. "Am I keeping you from something?"

I was desperately looking over his shoulder, trying to see where Elizabeth had gone. It must have seemed quite rude.

I shook my head. "Sorry, no."

By now, even Grandma Grant and Jess were looking at me with puzzled frowns on their faces.

Joe finally tapped his pen on his pad and frowned. "Okay. That'll be all for now. Can I take your address, in case we need to question you further?"

Grandma waved a hand at him. "There's no need for that. Chief Wickham knows where we live." And with that, she bustled off, leaving Joe before he could contradict her.

"Sorry, about that," I said, desperate to stop him thinking our family was totally crazy.

I gave him our address, and he nodded slowly before walking off, but not without looking back at us suspiciously a couple of times.

"Crap," I said to Jess. "He thinks we're a family of nutjobs."

"Well, you didn't exactly help by gasping out like that in the middle of his questioning. What was all that about?"

"Elizabeth," I said miserably. "I saw her passing by just as Joe was starting to ask us questions, but I could hardly run off in the middle of it, could I?"

"No, I suppose not."

"I'd better go and look for her."

I had to put Joe out of my mind. I needed to find Elizabeth

fast. Hopefully, she could tell us who had killed her, and we could put an end to all this.

CHAPTER 7

Jess left me to look for Elizabeth alone. She couldn't exactly help since she didn't see ghosts, so I was better off looking on my own.

I made a circuit of all the stalls first. The tables had been set out in a semicircle. As I walked, I scanned the crowds of locals for any sign of Elizabeth.

Sometimes, it was possible to confuse a ghost for a real person. In certain lights, they would appear almost see-through. Other times, they could look as real as you or me.

I'd been looking for twenty minutes or so, and I was starting to despair of ever finding Elizabeth. I decided to have a quick look under one of the stalls. The bric-a-brac stall had a large, lace tablecloth draped over it, so I lifted it up and peered underneath.

I'm not really sure why I thought Elizabeth might be hiding

under there, but I soon regretted looking. When I dropped the tablecloth and started to straighten, I saw a pair of black boots in front of me. I cringed. I knew who they belonged to even before I looked up.

Honestly, if he didn't already think I was a complete nutcase, he definitely would now.

My eyes traveled slowly upwards taking in the blue jeans that fitted snugly around his legs and then up his broad chest until finally my gaze rested on that handsome face.

Unfortunately right now, that handsome face was creased with a frown.

"Looking for something, Miss Grant?"

I don't react well when flustered, and I was definitely flustered at that moment.

"I, um... I lost an earring. I was just looking for it."

Joe's frown deepened, and then he reached out a hand, gently touching the side of my face, and tilted my head to one side. "You seem to have both earrings in at the moment."

"I... I..." I stammered, dismissing the warm tingles that traveled over my body as some sort of witchy sense, a reaction to some bad energy in the air. I was sure it had nothing at all to do with the proximity of the dazzlingly handsome Joe McGrady.

My hand flew to my little gold earrings.

"Silly me," I said, grinning cheerfully, while inside I was groaning at my ridiculous behavior.

I blushed furiously as I stepped past Joe and walked on.

I'd pretty much given up on finding Elizabeth and had decided to head back home when I caught sight of her again.

She was standing beside Mrs. Townsend and chatting away. Mrs. Townsend didn't flinch or respond, clearly because she couldn't even see Elizabeth, let alone hear her.

I chewed on my lower lip for a second, hesitating. Elizabeth Naggington terrified me in real life, and as a ghost, I didn't think she was going to be any less formidable.

I stepped up to them and cleared my throat.

"Mrs. Townsend, Chief Wickham was just asking for you. He's over by the inflatable castle if you'd like to go and see him."

Mrs. Townsend nodded. "Thank you, Harper. It's a terrible business," she said as she walked off.

"How rude!" Elizabeth Naggington exclaimed. "We were in the middle of a conversation, Harper Grant. Did no one ever teach you any manners? Of course, I really couldn't expect better, with a grandmother like yours to lead you an example."

I felt my blood boil, and I was severely tempted to flounce off and leave her to deal with her new life as a ghost all on her own. But I managed to control my temper.

"Elizabeth," I whispered, hoping nobody else would overhear us. "I need to talk to you. It's terribly important. Could you meet me behind the vegetable tent?" I said, nodding towards the tent that held all the pumpkins that would now probably never be judged.

"Well, I never," Elizabeth Naggington said, haughtily.

She floated along beside me as I walked over to the vegetable tent. When I was sure we were hidden behind the large white tarpaulin, I turned to Elizabeth and braced myself.

"Elizabeth, you need to listen to me."

"I need to do no such thing. Something very strange is going on out there. A body has been found in a barrel. It's quite extraordinary. I can't waste my time here talking to you. I need to go and find out what's happened."

As Elizabeth began to float off, I reached out my hand.

Unfortunately, you can't actually touch a ghost, so my hand just went right through her.

Elizabeth did a double take and then stared fiercely at me. "What did you just do?"

"Elizabeth, I need to speak to you about the body in the barrel."

"What about it?"

Elizabeth clearly had no idea she was a ghost. This was majorly awkward.

There was nothing for it. I just had to come out with the truth.

"It was your body in the barrel, Elizabeth."

Elizabeth put her hands on her hips. "What are you going on about, Harper? You really are a very strange young woman."

I ignored Elizabeth's insults. This couldn't be an easy transition for her, and I was determined to be as understanding as I could in the circumstances.

"Elizabeth, they found your body in the apple bobbing barrel."

Elizabeth stared blankly at me for a few moments. I didn't know whether she was processing the information, or simply shocked into silence, but after a moment, she said, "Me in the barrel? Don't be so ridiculous, Harper. If it was me, how can I be standing here now having a conversation with you?"

"I don't suppose you noticed," I said. "But you're not exactly standing. You're hovering about a foot off the ground."

Elizabeth's eyes widened, and she looked down at the floor and gave a little gasp when she saw her feet were not in contact with the floor.

"What? What have you done?"

"I haven't done anything, Elizabeth. You're a ghost. You've been killed. I'm ever so sorry."

"No! I can't have been killed."

I took that as evidence Elizabeth didn't remember being killed, which meant she wouldn't remember her killer either, which gave us a problem.

"You're talking utter rubbish, Harper Grant. You shouldn't joke about such horrible things." And with that, Elizabeth hovered off.

I followed her as she floated around, talking to people. When none of them responded, I saw that the cold, hard truth was slowly sinking in.

Eventually, she returned to my side. "So, you're the only one who can see me?"

I nodded sadly. "I'm afraid so."

I heard Jess's voice behind me. "Who are you talking to?"

"I found her," I told Jess, looking pointedly at Elizabeth.

Jess's mouth formed a silent oh as she looked at the spot where Elizabeth was, even though I knew Jess couldn't really see her.

"Can you see me?" Elizabeth asked anxiously, looking at Jess.

I shook my head. "She can't see you or hear you."

Elizabeth's shoulders slumped.

And then suddenly she seemed to find a wealth of energy from somewhere.

"Hang on a minute. Who killed me? Who had the audacity to dare...?" She spun around in a circle as if her killer would suddenly appear, and she could give them a good telling off.

"We don't know that yet. I was hoping you might remember."

Elizabeth's forehead puckered up in a frown as she thought hard. "I don't remember."

"What's the last thing you do remember?"

"Well, I remember eating that horrible lunch at the diner," she said.

I rolled my eyes. Since I was the only human who could actually see her, I had thought she might try and be a little nicer to me. Obviously, I'd been mistaken.

"I remember going home and talking to Robert and Robert Jr, but after that, it's a bit hazy."

I felt that same tingling sensation I'd experienced earlier and looked up. Standing a few feet away, Joe McGrady was staring at me.

My cheeks grew hot, and I stared down at the ground. I was going to have to be careful with him. He had clearly worked out that there was something different about us, and I could tell it wouldn't be easy to hide things from him.

"I think we can go now we've been questioned," I said to Jess. "Come on, Elizabeth, you'd better come home with us."

When I spoke, I kept my eyes fixed on Jess, so that Joe, or anybody else watching, would think I was just talking to her.

"Well, I don't want to come back with you," Elizabeth said, folding her arms across her chest. "I want to go back to my own house."

I sighed. This was not going to be easy.

CHAPTER 8

"You should be ashamed of yourself, Harper Grant!" Elizabeth snapped. "This is nothing but a mean trick. I don't know how you've managed to persuade everybody to play along with your little game, but I will not stand for it."

Elizabeth whirled around in mid-air and floated away.

I groaned. That was all I needed. A ghost with attitude. I should have guessed that Elizabeth Naggington would make a terrible ghost.

I'd started to move after her when Jess put a hand on my arm. "What's wrong?"

I leaned closer to my sister. "Elizabeth doesn't believe she's a ghost. She thinks I'm trying to trick her."

"Give her a chance to think things through. It can't be easy being told something like that."

My sister had always been the kind, understanding one. I was the one who liked to charge ahead and get everything organized, but in this case, Jess was definitely right.

Elizabeth didn't trust me, and she needed to think things through herself. I needed to give her space.

"But what if she gets into trouble?" I said, staring after Elizabeth's disappearing form.

Jess shrugged. "How much trouble can she get in? She's a ghost."

I nodded. "Good point."

"She knows where we live. Once she realizes that you were telling her the truth and that you're actually the only one she can talk to, I'm sure she'll come and find us."

I nodded again. Jess was right. Elizabeth would come and find me when she was good and ready.

Until then, we had a murderer on the loose in our tiny town.

I shivered and linked arms with Jess as we set off in search of Grandma Grant. We caught sight of her talking to Chief Wickham.

"But what are we going to do about the pumpkins? I spent ever such a long time growing mine. They don't get to that size and quality on their own, you know. It takes a special kind of talent to get them that big."

Poor Chief Wickham looked thoroughly worn out. I was sure it had more to do with Grandma Grant chewing his ear off than having to deal with the first murder case of his career.

"Come on, Grandma," I said, reaching out and slipping my arm under hers. "Let's go home and let Chief Wickham get on with his job."

I couldn't see Joe, but I didn't look too hard. Every time I saw him, I did something awkward or silly and made a fool of myself.

Chief Wickham looked very glad to see me. "Oh, Harper and Jess! Make sure your grandmother gets home safe."

"Do you have any idea who was responsible yet?" I asked.

Chief Wickham shook his head. "Not yet, but you girls don't have to worry. Joe and I will soon have whoever is responsible locked up."

Together the three of us trudged back to Grandma Grant's house.

The fall breeze was sharp today. The sky was blue, and the leaves on the trees were bright orange. Leaves crunched under our feet as we walked.

"I do hope Elizabeth is going to be all right," I said.

Grandma Grant turned to me and raised an eyebrow. "You've changed your tune. Before we got to the festival, you were begging us to put a spell on her."

I gave a little huff of annoyance. "I wanted a spell to make the festival finish quickly. I didn't want anything bad to happen to Elizabeth. And I certainly didn't want anyone to murder her."

"Well," Grandma Grant said, raising an eyebrow. "You didn't try to put a spell on her yourself, did you?"

My jaw dropped open, and I slipped my arm from hers, turning to her in disgust. "How could you even ask such a thing? Do you really think I wanted her dead?"

Grandma Grant shook her head. "No, of course not, but you've never been very good with spells. It wouldn't surprise me if you'd messed one up."

I was rendered speechless, which was probably a good thing. Otherwise, I would have said something I regretted later.

Jess stepped in between us, grabbing our hands and pulling us up the hill. "Now, come on. Let's not argue. Of course, Harper didn't put a spell on Elizabeth."

"Thank you, Jess," I said, looking pointedly at Grandma Grant. "At least one of you has faith in me."

"Oh, it's not that," Jess said breezily. "I just know you wouldn't have the first idea where to start if you wanted to cast a spell on Elizabeth."

I stared at Jess in disbelief. Honestly, there was nothing like a supportive family was there? And my family was nothing like a supportive one.

ONCE INSIDE THE HOUSE, we sat around the kitchen table with mugs of chamomile tea, one of Grandma Grant's specialties. She may have been a bad cook, but she was fantastic at making herbal teas and tinctures.

The chamomile tea was calming, and my urge to murder

Grandma Grant and Jess had just about passed. Athena jumped onto my lap and curled up as I stroked her soft, black fur.

I was just starting to relax when Elizabeth Naggington floated in through the kitchen wall.

You might think I would be used to that sort of thing by now, but it's not really something you ever get used to.

I jolted in my chair, spilling the chamomile tea and burning my fingers as the liquid sloshed onto the table. Athena gave a yelp and jumped off of my lap.

"Careful, Harper!" Grandma Grant said, leaning over with a cloth to mop up the mess.

But my eyes were fixed on the spot above Grandma Grant's head where Elizabeth was floating high above us.

Her ghostly face was streaked with tears, and she was sobbing.

Jess followed my gaze and frowned. "Is she back?"

"Yes," I said.

"Well, that didn't take long. I thought she'd flounce around for a few hours before finally coming to her senses," Grandma Grant said, which made Elizabeth stop crying and shoot her an angry glare.

"How dare she!" Elizabeth said. "Do you not have any respect for the dead?"

"She can't hear you, Elizabeth," I reminded her.

Athena had cautiously returned to her spot on my lap and looked up at the exact spot where Elizabeth was hovering. I guessed animals were a little more perceptive than humans when it came to ghosts.

Elizabeth pursed her lips in annoyance and looked back at me.

"So, you are right. I am a ghost. I hope that makes you happy. I tried to talk to Robert, and he just walked right through me."

Although she was trying to sound angry, I could see the sadness in Elizabeth's eyes and felt sorry for her.

"So," Elizabeth said with a shrug. "What do I do now?"

"I'm not exactly an expert," I said. "But in my experience, people who are ghosts hang around for a reason. Usually, they have some unfinished business, sometimes an unrequited love, or a very strong attachment to family, so they don't want to let go. In your case, Elizabeth, I think it's because somebody killed you, and until we find out who was responsible, and they're appropriately punished, I think you're going to remain here as a ghost."

"And what happens afterward? If we do find out who killed me, what happens to me then?"

I shook my head. "That, I don't know. But I think you pass on to the other side."

Elizabeth was silent as she pondered on that for a moment and then said, "Right. First things, first. We need to find out who killed me. So, where do we start?"

I was a little taken aback at Elizabeth's quick change in mood.

She'd gone from a crying mess to possessing a businesslike, brisk efficiency, and it made my head spin.

"Well," I began tentatively. "I suppose we look for some clues, and try and find out who would have benefited from your death."

Jess, who was sitting beside me, and keeping up with my side of the conversation, piped up, "Yes, did she have a will? Maybe Elizabeth's husband inherits a fortune."

Elizabeth's jaw hung open. And she opened and shut her mouth a couple of times like a goldfish. "Of all the rude things to say! Robert adored me. He couldn't be the one who killed me."

I didn't say anything. I'm not quite sure adored would be the right word to describe Robert's feelings towards his wife.

From the way I'd seen him treated over the last few years at the diner, I imagined at times he was quite frustrated by his wife.

Still, there was no need to be unkind, so instead of pointing that out, I just said, "Can you think of anybody else who might have benefited from your death, or anybody else who would want to kill you?"

Elizabeth's face creased up in concentration, and then she held up a finger, and her face lit up, "I know! I know exactly who did it."

I thought she'd remembered something, so I leaned forward eagerly and said, "Who? Who did it?"

Elizabeth folded her arms over her chest and nodded. "Yes, of course, it all makes sense now."

"What does?" I asked, growing exasperated.

As she was a ghost, I couldn't exactly shake the information out of her, even though I would have liked to.

"Well, think about it," she said. "Who did I annoy today? Through absolutely no fault of my own, of course. I was just telling the truth."

I frowned. "Who?"

"Archie, of course. Did you see his face when I criticized the food at the diner?"

I leaned back in my seat and sighed. For a moment, I had really believed Elizabeth had remembered something.

I shook my head. "That's ridiculous. Archie is not a killer."

"Archie?" Grandma Grant repeated and then snorted with laughter. "Honestly, I never heard something so ridiculous. That man couldn't hurt a fly."

Elizabeth looked quite put out. "If you're just going to laugh at me, then I won't say anything at all."

She pursed her lips as if to show she was determined to live up to her promise to keep silent.

But I wasn't really worried. I knew she couldn't keep it up. Elizabeth Naggington wasn't the type to stay quiet for long.

"I tell you what," I said. "This evening, we'll take a little walk around town and see if anything jogs your memory."

Elizabeth nodded. "I suppose we could do that. But what am I going to do in the meantime?"

"Hang around here, I guess."

"Why can't we go now?"

"Because I'm going to go with you, and I can't talk to you with other people around. I don't need the rest of the town thinking I'm completely off my rocker. We'll go tonight when it's dark."

Elizabeth huffed out a breath, and then she floated downwards and tried to sit down beside Grandma Grant. Unfortunately, she hadn't quite gotten the hang of it yet and slipped right through the chair.

I put a hand against my mouth and smothered my laughter, earning me a glare from Elizabeth.

"Honestly," she said. "Out of all the people in this town, I can't believe I can only talk to you."

CHAPTER 9

I DECIDED to go outside into the yard and try and tackle some of the weeds in the flower bed beside the greenhouse, but Elizabeth wasn't content to wait until later. She made herself bothersome, hovering over my shoulder until I finally relented.

It didn't seem as if I was going to get any peace.

"Fine! We'll go and look for some clues now," I said. "We'll go back to the field and see if anything there triggers your memory. How's that?"

Elizabeth gave me a smug smile. "I'm glad you finally got your priorities straight. Finding my killer really is a great deal more important than pulling up a few dandelions, after all."

After I'd washed up, we headed back down to the school field.

It was abandoned, but most of the stalls were still in place and covered with crime scene tape so we couldn't get too close.

Keith Tucker, who worked part-time for the police department, was standing beside the gate to the field entrance. He looked ever so pleased with himself.

"Hello, Harper. I'm afraid I can't let you go any closer. This is a crime scene." He puffed himself up self-importantly.

"Hello, Keith, do you know if the police have discovered anything else yet?"

Keith looked very happy to be asked. "I'm afraid I can't possibly talk about the case to a civilian." He tucked his thumbs in his belt hoops.

"That boy needs taking down a peg or two," Elizabeth said.

I looked meaningfully in the direction of the field, hoping that Elizabeth would get my hint and go off by herself to have a look and see if anything triggered her memory.

Just because I couldn't go, didn't mean Elizabeth couldn't. Keith Tucker couldn't see Elizabeth, after all.

Unfortunately, Elizabeth didn't take the hint. So I widened my eyes as I looked at her and then nodded towards the field.

She looked at me blankly.

"Are you okay there, Harper?" Keith said, frowning, obviously concerned at the fact I was nodding towards what looked like a blank space.

"Yes, fine. I thought I'd just stay here and have a little chat with you. It must get ever so boring standing guard like this."

I jerked my thumb, and finally, Elizabeth seemed to get the hint.

"Oh, why didn't you say so, Harper," she said. "I'll go over to the field, and see if I can see anything while you keep this annoying young man busy."

Finally.

Keith was still looking at me suspiciously.

"So, no leads yet then, Keith?"

Keith opened his mouth as if to answer, and then grinned and shook his head. He wagged a finger at me. "Nice try. You almost got me there, but I can't talk—"

"—to a civilian, I know," I said. "How long have you been standing here? You must be cold."

"Oh, I don't mind. It's a very important job, after all. They wouldn't trust just anybody to do it."

I nodded "True. It's obviously a reflection of how much Chief Wickham trusts you."

Elizabeth hovered back over to us. "Nothing," she said miserably.

That was fast. Although I couldn't say I was actually enjoying my conversation with Keith Tucker and was pretty glad we could leave.

"Right, I'd better leave you to it. I don't want to distract you from the job." I smiled at Keith.

He beamed back at me happily.

After we had walked a safe distance away, and I could talk to Elizabeth without anyone overhearing and thinking I was crazy, I turned to her and said, "You didn't spend very long looking. You were so eager to leave the house, and then you spent less than a minute looking around the field."

"When you know, you just know. I can't remember anything about the field. There was nothing there that triggered my memory. I don't think I was killed there."

"And do you have any idea where you were killed?"

Elizabeth shook her head sadly.

I really did want to help Elizabeth. It couldn't be pleasant for her hanging around the community and not be able to communicate with anyone apart from me.

"Let's go and talk to Chief Wickham. He might be able to give us some information that could help."

Elizabeth nodded morosely. "All right."

As we walked along Main Street towards the police station, I warned Elizabeth, "Now, when we're inside. I need you to keep quiet. I can't have you distracting me. If I answer you, or react to you in any way, I look like a complete crazy person. Remember that."

Unfortunately, when I turned away from Elizabeth, I was greeted with the sight of Mrs. Townsend walking towards us. She had a very perplexed expression on her face.

I plastered on a smile and carried on walking.

When Mrs. Townsend was out of earshot, I turned to Elizabeth and hissed, "See, that's the kind of funny look I get when people see me talking to thin air."

Elizabeth casually looked over her shoulder. "Oh, don't worry about her. At the last book club, she put forward Fifty Shades of Grey as the next book for us to read! If she spreads any rumors about you, you can retaliate with that little chestnut. That will soon shut her up."

"I don't want to retaliate. I just want people to think I'm normal," I said, but I couldn't resist looking over my shoulder at the diminutive, grey-haired Mrs. Townsend.

Fifty shades of Grey? Really?

"Now, behave," I warned Elizabeth again as we reached the door to the police station.

Abbott Cove's police station is tiny. It's made up of only three offices, and one tiny jail block tagged on the back.

They didn't even have a receptionist most of the time, so I walked past the reception desk, which was empty, towards the wooden door, bearing the brass plaque with Chief Wickham's name on it.

Before I could knock, the door opened, but it wasn't Chief Wickham staring down at me, it was Joe McGrady.

I supposed I shouldn't really have been surprised to see him since he did work there.

"Hello, again," he said. "Can I help you?" He was holding a

mug of coffee and leaned back against the door frame, looking at me suspiciously.

"Yes, actually you can," Elizabeth said behind me. "You can stop sitting around here, sipping coffee, and go and find my killer!"

I tried my best to ignore Elizabeth, but it really wasn't easy.

I smiled up at Joe. "I just popped in to see Chief Wickham."

Joe stepped aside and opened the door for me. Those sparkling blue, suspicious eyes didn't leave me for a second.

Chief Wickham looked up from his desk. "Oh, Harper. I hope nothing's wrong?"

"Nothing's wrong," I said, walking into his office and hoping Joe would leave us alone.

Joe McGrady made me nervous, which made me more apt to make a mistake and speak aloud to Elizabeth.

"I was hoping to find out how you are getting on with the investigation. You know Grandma Grant lives alone, and it's not nice to think a killer is lurking in our little town."

Chief Wickham gestured for me to sit down in the seat opposite his desk, and as I did so, he said, "Yes. It's making everyone nervous. We're not used to cases like this in Abbott Cove."

The chief's cheeks were flaming red, and his gray hair stood on end as he raked his hands through it in frustration just as the phone rang.

"Excuse me, Harper. I need to take this."

"Of course."

I hadn't realized Joe was still in the room, so when he leaned down and whispered in my ear, sending a wave of tingles along my skin, I jumped.

"The chief is fuming. They want to send out the state police to handle the investigation, and he is taking it as a personal affront."

"Thanks for the warning," I said in a low voice.

Joe left us to it, closing the door behind him just as Chief Wickham slammed down the telephone.

"They're sending a police investigator. What do they think I am? Chopped liver? I'll show them, Harper. You see if I don't. I'll solve the case before the investigator even gets here."

"I'm sure you will, Chief Wickham. If anyone can, you can."

Maybe I was overdoing the compliments a little.

"I wondered," I began. "Was Elizabeth murdered in the school field? I mean, I didn't see any blood so —"

I was asking because I thought if we could find the site of Elizabeth's murder, it could trigger her memory.

Chief Wickham walked around his desk and placed his ample backside on the corner of the desk.

"There wasn't much blood," he said. "She was strangled with a piece of wire."

"Strangled!" Elizabeth practically screamed the word. "Oh, oh....I think I'm going to faint."

As she began to fall backward, my arm shot out as I tried to save her, but then my hand froze in mid-air, and I clasped my hands together and put them in my lap.

Elizabeth couldn't faint. She was a ghost. And even if she did and fell on the floor, it wasn't going to hurt her.

"I was trying to swat a fly," I said to Chief Wickham by way of an explanation.

He was staring at me, his eyes wide with surprise.

"Do you think whoever strangled her was local?" I asked.

Chief Wickham shook his head. "I know you're concerned, Harper. We all are. But I can't talk about the ongoing investigation with you, I'm afraid. When I have news to share, I'll let the whole community know. But you can rest assured I'm on the case."

The chief winked at me.

I guess that was it then. That was all I could do for now. I wasn't going to get any more answers from the chief, but at least we now knew how Elizabeth had been murdered.

Elizabeth was lying on the floor, sprawled out dramatically, but when I stood up and didn't pay her any attention, she opened one eye.

"Well, honestly. I can't believe the lack of sympathy I get," she muttered as she picked herself up from the floor and followed me out of Chief Wickham's office.

CHAPTER 10

"WHAT DO WE DO NOW?" Elizabeth asked me. Her shoulders were slumped as she hovered from side to side, looking very upset.

"I suppose we keep looking for clues," I said. "We need something to jog your memory. Perhaps we should go to your house?"

"My house? I can tell you for certain I wasn't killed there. Since my Robert retired, we've been inseparable. Nobody would have dared try to strangle me at home."

"Still, maybe familiar surroundings could trigger something?"

To be honest, I couldn't think of anywhere else we could go.

Elizabeth nodded. "Well, I would like to go home. Although I'm sure it will be very upsetting to see Robert and Robert Jr so distraught over my passing. They must be missing me terribly."

We took a right on Main Street and headed back into the residential section behind the library.

Elizabeth's house was on Wisteria Avenue, which was lined with a collection of one-story houses, built twenty-five years ago when the town had expanded.

All of the front lawns were carefully manicured, and people in this neighborhood took pride in maintaining their houses to an impeccable standard.

"Here we are." Elizabeth beamed as we stopped beside a white picket fence. "What are you going to do, Harper? Are you going to knock?"

I stuffed my hands in the pockets of my jeans. I should have thought of that. I should have brought a casserole or something and offered my condolences.

But then again, Robert had seen Elizabeth fly off the handle over my inability to serve her iced tea promptly, so I wasn't sure whether he would consider my condolences genuine.

"Perhaps I could just stand out here," I said. "You go and take a look inside."

"Well, if you're sure."

Mr. Townsend chose that moment to walk past with his little Pomeranian.

He tipped his hat to me, and wished me good afternoon, as I leaned down to pet the dog.

Elizabeth happily hovered up to the front door. Instead of just floating through, which of course she could do now that she was a ghost, she peered in through the window, which I guessed must be giving her a view into the kitchen.

As Mr. Townsend and his dog walked away, Elizabeth let out a bloodcurdling shriek.

I raced up the driveway to join her. "What's wrong?" I whispered urgently.

But Elizabeth was too distraught to answer. She pointed at the window.

I looked inside, but I didn't see anything terrible. I couldn't see anything that could have upset her so badly.

Robert Naggington was wearing an apron and standing beside the stove. Next to him on the counter, he had a variety of different spices, and a strong smell was wafting through the window.

I turned back to Elizabeth and shook my head, trying to keep myself hidden behind the frilly, white curtains.

"What is the matter?"

This time, Elizabeth Naggington found her voice. "He is cooking a curry!"

I nodded. "And?"

Elizabeth widened her eyes as if she couldn't believe I was being so thickheaded.

"Robert knows he isn't allowed to cook curry in the house. The smell will linger for days!"

I raised an eyebrow, opened my mouth and then closed it again. If I reminded Elizabeth Naggington of the fact she was now dead and wouldn't be bothered by the smell of the curry in the house, it would be a little insensitive.

At just that moment, Elizabeth's son stepped into the kitchen.

He looked very like his father, only a little broader and about twenty pounds overweight.

"Ah, Robert Jr!" Elizabeth beamed with pleasure at the sight of her son. "He'll sort this out. Just you watch, Harper. He'll tell his father to stop it immediately. He knows they're not allowed to cook curry."

But instead of saying anything of the sort to his father, Robert Jr walked over to the refrigerator and took out two bottles of beer. He handed one to his father and smiled.

Father and son popped open their beers, clinked the bottles together, and both took a long swallow straight from the bottles.

I thought Elizabeth was going to have a choking fit. "No, don't drink out of the bottle! Get a glass!"

I could hear Robert's muffled voice from where I stood hidden by the frilly yellow curtains around the kitchen window. "I'm cooking a curry, son. Would you like some?"

"No!" Elizabeth shouted. "Tell him no! Tell him he is expressly forbidden from cooking anything like that in my kitchen!"

"Thanks, Dad. That smells great."

Elizabeth's jaw fell open as she hovered by the window gaping at the scene.

I didn't think watching them was helping. It wasn't providing any clues as to who killed Elizabeth, and Robert and his son were obviously reveling in their newfound freedom, which was hurtful for Elizabeth to see.

"Come on," I said. "This isn't much help. Let's try something else."

"But they're eating curry!" Elizabeth whined.

"I know, but there's nothing we can do about it now, is there? Let's try something else."

I walked away, hoping that Elizabeth would follow me. Luckily she did.

I shoved my hands in the pockets of my jeans as I walked down the driveway and sighed. I didn't know what to try next.

"I can't believe it," Elizabeth muttered as she floated along beside me. "I've only been dead a day. I expected them to show a little more respect than that. You know, now that I think about it, I'm sure Robert cooked curry when I was away visiting my sister in Australia. I was sure I could smell something when I returned home, but Robert told me I was imagining things. Of all the sneaky, rotten—"

I tried to change the subject to keep Elizabeth's mind off it.

"Well, what should we try next? We still need clues if we are going to find out who killed you."

Elizabeth shrugged. She had lost interest in the hunt for her killer and was far more interested in what spices Robert had been using.

"I always had to cook him the blandest food due to his poor digestion, but did you see how much chili powder he added to the pan? Well, he'll be suffering the effects later, mark my words, Harper."

As I couldn't rely on Elizabeth to come up with any theories, the only chance I had of helping her, was to come up with one of my own.

"What would you usually be doing this evening?"

"You mean if I wasn't a ghost?"

I nodded.

"I'd be at the book club in the church hall," Elizabeth said sadly. "We were going to be talking about a Nicholas Sparks book this evening."

"Right," I said. "Well, let's go there now and see if we can find anything that can help us work out what happened to you."

Elizabeth gave me a sideways glance. I think she was starting to doubt my investigative skills. I couldn't say I blamed her. I just hoped that Chief Wickham and Joe McGrady were having more luck than me and discovered her killer soon, so Elizabeth could find closure and move on.

"They've probably canceled it out of respect," Elizabeth said pointedly. "I imagine they are too upset to go ahead as if nothing had happened."

"Perhaps," I said and bit down on my lower lip. Elizabeth certainly had a distorted view of how people saw her. "Why don't we give it a try? They may have decided to go ahead as a way to remember you."

Elizabeth thought about that for a moment and then nodded. "I suppose you could be right."

She didn't sound convinced.

CHAPTER 11

WE REACHED the church hall just as dusk was falling.

We followed the winding path, which snaked through the graveyard and led to the church hall, which was a small wooden construction tagged on to the back of the church.

The wind had picked up, and orange and red leaves swirled about us.

"Heaven knows what book they'll pick next without me to guide them," Elizabeth said. "Honestly, some of their previous suggestions were really quite questionable."

As we walked around the side of the church, we could see that the lights were on and shining out from the church hall windows.

"Maybe I should go in, introduce myself and ask some questions?" I said.

I hadn't enjoyed peering in through the kitchen window of Elizabeth's old house. I kept imagining someone was about to tap me on the shoulder and demand to know why I was spying on a grieving widower. The last thing I wanted was to get caught spying on the Abbott Cove book club.

"Yes, perhaps." Elizabeth sounded distracted, which was odd for someone trying to track down her killer.

I expected her to be a little more interested in the investigation.

"But before you go in, let me just have a quick listen to the potential books they're discussing for next week."

Elizabeth sped off, and I sighed, trying to follow her quietly.

I had no idea how I would explain myself if someone found me crouching beside the church hall window.

When I reached Elizabeth's side and ducked beneath the windowsill, I was surprised to see her face was tense.

"What is it?" I whispered.

She flapped her hands at me to get me to shut up, and I realized she'd overheard something said by the ladies inside that she didn't particularly like.

I straightened up and tried to peek through the window.

Most of the women gathered around in a small circle in the center of the church hall, I recognized. They all had books on their laps, but rather than talking about the actual stories, they were having a good old gossip... about Elizabeth Naggington...

"I wouldn't be surprised if it was her tongue that got her into trouble. She was always saying nasty things about people."

Those words came from Ethel Goodridge, a sweet, elderly woman, who was known in the neighborhood for making the best apple pie.

Mrs. Townsend spoke up next, "If you ask me, she brought it on herself."

Elizabeth gasped beside me. "Of all the low-down, nasty things to say… And besides, nobody did ask her."

Victoria Andrews, the former principal of Abbott Cove School, spoke up, holding the book up in the air. "I really do think we should get back to the matter in hand, ladies. It's really unkind to be speaking about poor Elizabeth like this."

"Yes, you tell them, Victoria," Elizabeth waved her fist in the air and turned to me with a smug smile on her face. "See, Harper, there are some good people left in Abbott Cove."

Unfortunately, though, nobody paid Victoria Andrews any attention.

Tabitha Grewark, leaned forward, her eyes gleaming, enjoying the salacious gossip. "I heard that someone finally got sick of her nasty, bullying ways. It looks as if she picked on the wrong person to bully…"

There was a hush around the group, followed by murmurs of agreement.

I turned to see how Elizabeth was coping with this. My mother had always told me that eavesdroppers never heard good things about themselves, but I doubted that would be much consolation for Elizabeth.

Before I could ask if she was okay, Elizabeth zoomed off, moving much faster than I could.

Ducking down and hoping that no one would hear or see me, I tried to chase after her.

It was growing dark and difficult to see, but I made my way around the graveyard until I finally saw Elizabeth in the far corner, underneath a cedar tree, sobbing.

I felt very sorry for her. This had been a cruel wake-up call. She really had no idea how her rudeness and bullying had affected people over the years.

I wrapped my arms around myself and hugged my coat against me tightly as the wind whipped my hair around. It was definitely getting chilly.

The leaves rustled beneath my feet as I walked over to join Elizabeth.

"Is that really how people see me?" she asked between sobs.

I held up my hand, ready to pat her on the shoulder in an attempt to comfort her when I remembered that I couldn't do that to a ghost.

I lowered my hand. "Elizabeth, try not to let it upset you. You can't change anything now. The important thing is to concentrate on finding who killed you so you can move on."

She turned to me with red-rimmed eyes. I hadn't realized ghosts could cry. "I thought they were my f...f... friends."

DANICA BRITTON

I sighed. No one liked to hear horrible things like that said about themselves, even if they were true.

"Hey," a voice behind me said.

I turned around so quickly, I stumbled. Talk about a guilty reaction.

It was Joe McGrady.

"Hi," I replied, looking around wildly for Elizabeth, who seemed to have vanished.

"Who were you talking to?" Joe asked.

Oh, darn, he'd heard me. How on earth was I going to get out of this one? But before I could think up an excuse, Joe's eyes drifted down to the gravestone beside my feet.

"Ah, apologies. I just saw someone moving about in the churchyard and thought I'd better investigate, what with the murder and everything." He nodded at the gravestone. "I'm sorry. Someone close? Your parents?"

I finally got his meaning. He thought I'd been standing here talking to some dearly departed family member.

I looked down at the gravestone. Frederick Burton. Elizabeth's father.

"Er, no. My parents are both alive and well and living in New York City."

Joe frowned and then peered closely, so he could read the name on the gravestone. "Frederick Burton?"

Of course, Joe was a detective, and he would have made sure

76

he knew the names of Elizabeth's family. Standing by the grave of Elizabeth's father, linked me to her, and that wasn't a good thing. If Joe put two and two together, it might make him even more suspicious of me than he already was.

I nodded. "Er...Yes, good, old Fred."

"You knew him well?"

Truthfully, I'd only met Fred Burton twice, during visits to Grandma Grant's when I was a child. Fred had been elderly then, and by the time I moved to Abbott Cove, he'd already passed away.

I shrugged. "Sure, he was a lovely man." I tried to recall something about Fred to prove I knew him. "He grew huge summer squash."

Joe McGrady raised an eyebrow and looked slightly taken aback. I cringed.

Summer squash. Really, Harper? Really? That was the best you could come up with?

My cheeks were burning in mortification as Joe regarded me steadily. I had no excuse for blurting that out, except it was all I could remember about him. Grandma Grant had been very impressed by Fred Burton's squash, and determined to find out his secret, which had turned our vacation into a very eventful one.

She'd taken one of the squash to study, and Fred had arrived at her house accusing Grandma Grant of theft. Grandma denied it, of course, and I don't think my father ever got to the bottom of it.

77

DANICA BRITTON

After several awkward moments of silence, Joe finally said, "Do you want me to walk you home, Harper? It's dark, and after everything that's happened today, I don't think it's a good idea to be hanging around in a graveyard."

Now, normally being escorted home in the moonlight by a man as handsome as Joe McGrady would have been very appealing, but I was stuck. I had no idea where Elizabeth had disappeared to, and I didn't want to leave her behind, especially in the state she was in.

I tried to casually look behind him, only to fail spectacularly.

He turned his head. "What? Did you see something?"

I was really fed up of this. For once, I wished I could just be a normal woman.

Why couldn't I take advantage of this situation and flirt with the gorgeous Joe McGrady instead of worrying about a traumatized ghost who had just overheard her so-called friends bad-mouthing her?

Elizabeth Naggington hadn't been very nice to me when she was alive, and now that she was dead, she was still a thorn in my side.

I'd had enough. If Elizabeth wanted my help again, she could come and find me.

So I smiled brightly up at Joe and linked my arm through his. "Thank you, Joe, that would be very nice."

Joe nodded with a puzzled frown on his face, and then he escorted me out of the graveyard like a gentleman.

78

CHAPTER 12

I WISHED I was the type to have a dozen witty observations on hand so I could dazzle Joe with my conversation, but that really wasn't me.

I wasn't used to flirting, so my attempts to get Joe talking were pretty dismal.

"Any new developments on the murder?"

Joe shook his head. "Not really, although we have worked out what the murder weapon was."

"Chief Wickham said she'd been strangled with a piece of wire?"

Joe nodded. "Yes, she was strangled all right, but now we've identified the type of wire. It was cheese wire. It cut right into her skin."

I gulped and shivered. That was not a pretty picture.

I was glad Elizabeth wasn't around to hear it.

"Sorry," Joe said. "I shouldn't have said that. I didn't realize you were so close to the deceased."

"Oh, I wasn't really," I said.

"But, you knew her father very well?"

I stared at him and frowned. Temporarily forgetting he'd found me standing beside Fred Burton's grave.

For a moment, I wasn't quite sure what he was getting at, and then I realized.

He wasn't escorting me home because he was a gentleman, or because he was interested in me. He was trying to find out how closely I was related to the Naggington family.

He considered me a suspect.

That gave my confidence a serious knock and made me feel like a fool. I should have realized. Someone like Joe wouldn't be interested in a kooky witch like me.

I slipped my arm from his and nodded at him. "Thank you very much for making sure I got home safely, Deputy McGrady. I hope you catch the killer soon."

I shoved my hands in the pockets of my jeans and began to walk off quickly. I wasn't far from Grandma Grant's, there was only a short distance along the overgrown garden path to navigate.

"But you're not home yet, Harper," Joe called after me. "If you'll just wait a minute…"

"Thank you, but I'm fine," I said as I stomped up the garden path to Grandma Grant's house.

I STEPPED into Grandma's kitchen, and the warmth enveloped me. Athena was curled up in a chair, sound asleep. There was a fire burning in the old-fashioned fireplace, and Grandma Grant had a great big pot on the stove. She was stirring the contents with a wooden spoon.

When she heard me behind her, she jumped and dropped the wooden spoon into the liquid.

"Darn it, Harper!" She pressed a hand to her chest. "What are you doing sneaking up on me like that?"

"I wasn't sneaking. I've just come to see you. And what's that?" I asked suspiciously, pointing at whatever she had simmering on the stove.

"None of your business," she said gruffly and tried to fish out the wooden spoon with a large fork.

I walked over to the stove and peered over her shoulder. I took a sniff. It didn't exactly smell bad, but I was pretty sure whatever it was she had in the pot wasn't edible.

It was bright yellow in color and chopped green leaves floated on the surface together with what looked like bundles of tiny twigs.

"What is it?" I asked again.

"Soup."

I put my hands on my hips and shook my head. "That is not soup. I take it this is part of what you've been hiding from us then?"

"Stuff and nonsense," Grandma Grant said. "It's soup, a new recipe I'm trying out."

I leaned in further and breathed in the thick vapor. "It doesn't smell like soup."

"What is this? You waltz into the kitchen, uninvited I might add, and then you criticize my cooking skills. Really, Harper, I think—"

Grandma's voice trailed away as I screamed and slapped a hand across my mouth, pointing at the bubbling liquid.

Grandma frowned. "For goodness sake, Harper. What's wrong with you now?"

Athena, roused from her slumber, gave an irritated meow and then curled back up and closed her eyes again.

"An eye," I squeaked. "I just saw an eye in there!"

I pointed down at a small, spherical object in the center of the pot.

"Oh, don't make such a fuss. It's just eye of newt. And, I'll have you know, the newt was already dead when I found it. Died of natural causes."

I looked at my Grandma incredulously. "No one puts eyes in soup. Not even you! You're making a potion. So tell me what's it for?"

"Can't a woman have a little bit of privacy?"

I shook my head. "Not when it's always Jess and me who have to contain the fallout from the aftermath of your spells and potions."

At that moment, Jess burst in through the door, bringing a swirl of leaves in with her.

She wiped her boots on the mat. "It's cold out there tonight. Any luck?" Jess asked, looking at me expectantly as she shrugged off her coat.

I shook my head. "No. We spied on Elizabeth's husband and her friends from the book club, but we didn't get any new information, and Elizabeth got really upset because they all seemed to be coping quite well without her."

Jess grimaced. "Yes, I can see how that could upset her. Is Elizabeth here now?"

I shook my head. "She flounced off in the graveyard, and then I got caught by Joe McGrady. He wanted to know who I'd been talking to and insisted on escorting me home."

Jess grinned at me. "Joe McGrady, eh? I wouldn't kick him out of bed."

"Jess!" both Grandma and I exclaimed at the same time.

"What?" Jess said, grinning. "You can't tell me you hadn't noticed how hot our new lawman is."

I shrugged. "He's all right, I suppose."

"So, did he ask you out?" Jess asked, sidling up to me and

nudging me in the ribs.

"No. He did not. And the only reason he wanted to walk me home was to quiz me because he saw me standing and chatting away right next to Elizabeth's father's grave, so now I'm sure he thinks I'm somehow related to Elizabeth's death."

Jess's enthusiasm fizzled away. "Oh, that is a shame. We don't get many hot guys here in the Cove."

"What are you talking about?" Grandma Grant protested as she continued to stir her gross potion on the stove. "The Cove has plenty of good-looking men. What about Patrick Carter, Seth Greenaway, and, of course, Brian McKellen?"

Both Jess and I turned to Grandma Grant in horror, and Jess said, "Grandma, all of those men are over fifty. I'm sure they were quite the catch in their day, but I think Harper and I would prefer a slightly younger man."

Grandma said, "Well, if you're going to be picky..." She shrugged and turned back to her potion.

I sat down at the kitchen table and sighed. "I am a bit worried about Elizabeth, actually. She overheard some nasty things her friends at the book club were saying about her. It can't have been pleasant."

Jess sat down opposite me and said. "I'm sure it wasn't, but Elizabeth did say plenty of nasty things herself while she was alive."

Elizabeth chose that moment to float through the wall. "Oh," she said huffily. "So you're all talking about me behind my back as well."

I groaned. "Elizabeth, I was worried about you. You shouldn't flounce off like that. We are supposed to be working as a team, trying to work out who killed you."

Elizabeth shrugged. "I saw you talking to that young police officer. He seemed rather keen on you, so I thought I'd give you a bit of privacy."

Elizabeth had a teasing grin on her face. I couldn't keep up with the change in her moods. It made me dizzy.

I shook my head. "Well, if you'd stuck around, you would have seen he wasn't keen on me as you put it. He was trying to find out about my relationship with your father."

"My father?" Elizabeth stared at me, puzzled.

"Yes, he wanted to know how well I knew him because he found me standing next to your father's grave, talking to you. But of course he couldn't see you, so he assumed… Well, I don't know what he assumed actually. But I do know he thought I was behaving extremely strangely."

"Nothing new there," Grandma Grant muttered.

I ignored her.

"Ah," Elizabeth said, nodding. "Yes, I can see how that would have been rather awkward."

Awkward wasn't the word.

Over the course of the day, I had managed to embarrass myself in front of the chief of police, his new deputy and goodness knows how many other people who had spotted me spying on Robert Naggington.

CHAPTER 13

ELIZABETH WAS MOPING. "I don't think we are ever going to find my killer. I'll just have to stay around here forever with only you to talk to."

Elizabeth looked distraught.

I wasn't particularly enamored with that idea either. I didn't say that, though. I'm not completely heartless.

"We will find out who did this, Elizabeth. It's just going to take a little time."

"Well, we haven't made much progress so far."

"Sure, we have," I said, trying to sound encouraging. "We have found out how you were killed."

"Strangled," Elizabeth said mournfully as she rubbed her throat.

I nodded. "Yes, and I found out from Joe that the killer used cheese wire."

"Cheese wire! Oh, my word!"

Elizabeth looked like she might be sick. I shuffled over to the side. I was pretty sure ghosts couldn't actually throw up, but I didn't want to take any chances.

"Is that significant? It could be a clue? Do you know anybody who has cheese wire?"

Elizabeth thought for a moment and then nodded. She turned to me with a cunning smile. "I know someone who used cheese wire."

I nodded eagerly. "Who?"

Elizabeth nodded to herself. "Yes, it is all making sense now. All the pieces of the puzzle are falling into place."

I waited with bated breath for her to reveal the killer.

"What is it?" Jess said beside me.

"The cheese wire has triggered a memory for Elizabeth. I think she knows who did it."

Jess's eyes widened, and she reached out to hold my hand. "Who?"

That was a very good question.

"Well, Elizabeth, are you going to tell us?" I asked.

"It's quite obvious. You can't see it because you're too close to him. It's Archie."

My excitement evaporated, and I slumped back into the chair before turning to Jess, "She doesn't really remember. She's still saying she suspects Archie."

"I don't know why you won't even consider it," Elizabeth said haughtily. "It makes perfect sense. Archie was furious at me for criticizing the diner and its food, and he has an abundant supply of cheese wire. I know for a fact he held the cheese and wine evening for the Women's Institute in the church hall last month, and he definitely had cheese wire to cut the cheese up into little pieces."

I sighed. Anyone who knew Archie would know he was completely incapable of murder. Even as riled up as he'd been by Elizabeth's rudeness, he would never have harmed her.

I shook my head. "Fine. It's definitely not Archie, but if it makes you feel better, I'll talk to him at work tomorrow."

Elizabeth nodded. "Good. I'm glad to see you're finally taking me seriously."

I got to my feet and stretched.

"Well, it's been a busy day. I'm going to go home and go to bed. Elizabeth, you're welcome to spend the night at our house."

"Do ghosts actually sleep?"

I shrugged. "I've no idea. I guess you'll find out this evening."

IT TURNED out that ghosts could sleep. Elizabeth hovered horizontally over the couch all night, and she only woke up when I walked past her to get breakfast.

She made a scandalized noise as I poured some cereal into a bowl.

"You shouldn't eat that," she said pointing to the cereal packet. "It's far too processed."

I ignored her and added extra cereal to the bowl.

"So, what are we going to do today?" Elizabeth said, still frowning at the cereal.

"I'm going to work. Afterward, we'll make a plan and decide what we're going to do next."

Elizabeth looked disappointed. "Well, can I come to the diner with you? We might be able to get some clues if Archie did it."

I shot Elizabeth a warning look. "You can come with me, but only if you promise to behave and keep quiet."

Elizabeth pressed a hand to her chest. "Me? When do I ever behave anything less than impeccably?"

Before I could make a smart reply, Jess walked into the kitchen yawning. "Pour me a bowl, would you?"

"Good grief," Elizabeth said.

I poured Jess a large bowl of cereal and pushed it across the counter toward her so she could top it up with a generous serving of milk. "Elizabeth doesn't approve of our breakfast choice."

Jess shrugged and crunched through a large mouthful of

cereal.

Jess wasn't a keen conversationalist when she'd just woken up. She wasn't really a morning person. Neither was I, to be honest. I preferred to wait until after I'd had my first cup of coffee before interacting with anyone, but Elizabeth hadn't really given me much choice this morning.

I walked the ten-minute journey to work with Elizabeth hovering beside me, chatting away and making snappy comments about the people we passed.

I had a feeling today was going to be a definite challenge. Trying to remember not to respond to Elizabeth was tricky.

I pushed open the door to the diner and saw Archie was already there, setting up for the morning.

I could hear Sarah singing in the kitchen and smiled as I breathed in the familiar scent of the bacon she already had frying in the pan.

"Morning," I said cheerily, walking over to the coffee machine and checking everything was working okay.

Archie had issues with technology, and he'd never gotten on well with this machine since we'd gotten it.

"Morning," Archie replied, but he didn't quite seem his normal, sunny self.

"Is everything okay?"

Archie sighed and looked out of the window. "I had a visit from Chief Wickham last night, along with that new officer."

"Joe? Joe McGrady?"

"Yes, and they were both ever so interested in the scene Elizabeth created when she last visited the diner. I think they might consider me a suspect," Archie said, turning to me and wringing his hands.

"That's ridiculous. No one could seriously consider you a suspect. They're asking everyone questions. Joe asked me questions last night, too."

Archie's face took on an expression of relief, and he let out a large sigh. "Really? Oh, that is good news."

I raised an eyebrow.

"Sorry, I meant it's good news that they haven't singled me out, not that it's good news you were questioned."

Elizabeth had been oddly quiet. It made me suspicious. I looked over my shoulder and saw Elizabeth hovering by the kitchen hatch.

"He's definitely got the look of a guilty man," Elizabeth declared.

I tried not to react, but it wasn't easy.

"Are you okay finishing up here?" Archie said. "The sugar pots need filling."

"Of course," I said, and Archie bustled off to the kitchen to help Sarah with prep work.

Suddenly, Elizabeth gave a shriek, making me jump and tip sugar all over table ten. She zoomed across the diner and hid behind me.

"What on earth...?" I turned in surprise, and then I realized Elizabeth had seen Loretta, the diner's resident ghost.

I really should have warned her about that.

CHAPTER 14

LORETTA MET my gaze and rolled her eyes. "Great. Do you think next time you could bring a male ghost? I'm not so keen on the shrieking females."

She said it as though I had a choice in the matter, but I managed to swallow my retort and turned to try and reassure Elizabeth.

"Elizabeth, meet Loretta. She's a ghost, too. I imagine you two will have lots to talk about."

When Elizabeth stopped crouching behind me, Loretta gave me a dirty look.

"I don't talk to newbies," she said, arching an eyebrow.

"Be nice, Loretta," I whispered. "You were a new ghost once."

"Hmm," Loretta said, looking Elizabeth up and down. "I'll give you five minutes."

Elizabeth looked fascinated by the sight of another ghost, and she followed Loretta to a table, her hands clasped together, absolutely enthralled.

I smiled as I attempted to clean up the spilled sugar. Hopefully, Loretta would keep Elizabeth out of my hair for a while.

Over the next hour, we only had a couple of customers, and Elizabeth did what she was told and kept quiet.

The only time I heard her was when old Bob went to sit in his normal seat by the window, sitting down directly on top of Elizabeth.

She squealed and flew up in the air, and it was all I could do not to laugh out loud. Loretta wasn't so kind. She guffawed loudly.

"How rude!" Elizabeth put her hands on her hips and glared at Bob, but of course, he was completely oblivious.

I ignored Elizabeth and Loretta as I walked over and gave Bob his coffee.

"Morning, Bob. The usual?" I asked.

Bob always had bacon, extra crispy, and two eggs, sunny side up.

"That would be lovely," Bob said.

Leaving Elizabeth standing beside the counter, grumbling to herself, I walked into the kitchen to give Sarah the order.

"Old Bob's here, Sarah, and he'd like his usual."

"Right you are," Sarah said and headed over to the stove.

"Are you okay, Sarah?"

Sarah was a sensible, stout woman. She had a gloriously beautiful head of red hair, which she always wore tightly pinned back and covered in the kitchen.

She turned to me and tried to smile, but I could see it was a struggle.

"I'm feeling a bit off kilter, to be honest. It was awful finding Elizabeth's body yesterday, and then last night, I had a thorough grilling from Chief Wickham and Joe McGrady. Chief Wickham is normally such a nice man, but he was ever so cold last night."

I leaned back on the kitchen counter. It was starting to sound as if Chief Wickham and Joe had questioned most of Abbott Cove last night.

"I suppose the chief has to do everything by the book. It's the first murder he's ever had to work, and he is under a lot of pressure."

Sarah nodded as she broke two eggs into the pan. "I suppose you're right. But I don't think that excuses rudeness."

"Rudeness?" Chief Wickham was an old-fashioned gentleman. I couldn't imagine him ever being rude to anyone.

"Yes, that new one, Joe McGrady. He was all charming and kind at first, and he got me to trust him, and then he asked the most impertinent questions!"

"Impertinent?"

Sarah looked behind us to make sure we were alone in the

kitchen. "He asked me if I'd been having an affair with Elizabeth's husband."

My eyes grew wide as I stared at Sarah. "You hadn't been, had you?"

Sarah shook her head vigorously. "No, of course not."

Elizabeth chose that moment to float through the door.

"What's going on in here? Do we suspect Sarah now? She was ever so upset when I criticized her cooking," Elizabeth said and floated right up to Sarah, hovering in front of her face, but Sarah didn't bat an eyelid.

A loud bang sounded from the storeroom, a large room just off the kitchen where Archie stored the diners' supplies.

"What on earth was that?" I asked.

Sarah shrugged and rolled her eyes. "It's Archie. He's in ever such a funny mood today. I think he's decided to rearrange some boxes in there."

I peered out of the kitchen hatch to make sure that none of the customers needed service, and when I saw that everyone was happily sipping their coffee, I poked my head into the storeroom.

I couldn't see Archie at first, so I stepped a little further inside, and Elizabeth followed me.

Archie was bent over at the waist with his butt in the air as he rummaged through a large cardboard box.

"What are you doing, Archie?" I asked.

Archie shot up in the air and turned around, looking panicked and clutching something to his chest.

He looked absolutely terrified.

"What's that?" I asked, pointing to the object he was desperately trying to hide behind his back.

Archie's eyes looked down. "Oh, it's nothing. I was just doing a spot of spring cleaning."

"Archie, it's Fall, not Spring."

I stepped closer to Archie and saw exactly what he was trying to hide.

"Archie, is that cheese wire?"

Elizabeth began to fly around the storeroom. "I knew it! Didn't I tell you so, Harper? He did it! Quick, call the police."

Archie's lip wobbled a little. "Joe McGrady told me last night what weapon the killer used, and I knew I had a great bundle of it here. I thought it would make me look guilty, so I was trying to hide it. But it wasn't me, Harper. You have to believe that."

"Of course, I don't think it was you," I said and patted his shoulder.

"What? Are you crazy?" Elizabeth screamed. "He just practically admitted it. The man is clearly a cold-blooded killer!"

"Hey!" I shouted at Elizabeth.

Archie looked puzzled. "What?"

I flushed, realizing that I'd spoken to Elizabeth out loud in front of Archie.

"Er, I thought I saw a mouse."

I was terrible at making up excuses on the spot.

"What!" Archie squealed in a high-pitched voice, his eyes frantically searching the floor.

"My mistake. I think it was just a shadow, Archie. Why don't you come into the kitchen and get a cup of coffee? I've got to get back to serve old Bob his breakfast."

Archie nodded, but he didn't stop searching the floor for the mouse.

"I'll be along in a moment," he said.

I moved out of the storeroom, into the kitchen and collected old Bob's breakfast from Sarah. As I carried the plate through to the diner, Elizabeth snootily said, "I'm not surprised he has mice. It's only to be expected in a terrible place like this."

"Will you stop?" I hissed at Elizabeth. "I didn't see a mouse. I only said that to cover my reaction to you. I have quite enough problems, thank you very much, without my boss thinking I'm nuts."

I gave her a furious look and then pursed my lips together, determined not to speak to Elizabeth for the rest of my shift.

AFTER WORK, I was still thinking about Archie as I grabbed my coat and headed outside with Elizabeth following me closely.

"I don't know why you're so grouchy with me," she complained. "I'm the victim in all this."

I didn't respond and instead nodded to Mrs. Townsend as she passed us, walking her little Pomeranian.

When we turned the corner, I couldn't see anyone and so figured it was safe to speak. I said, "Elizabeth, I am not grouchy."

"Yes, you are, Harper. You haven't spoken to me all day."

I shook my head in disbelief. "Elizabeth, I can't talk to you because if I did, people would think I was crazy. Surely you can see that?"

Elizabeth shrugged. "I still think it's rude."

It had been a long day, and all I wanted to do was get home and have a nice hot bath, but I didn't know what I could do to help Elizabeth. I needed to do something soon, or she was going to drive me crazy.

I hoped that as time passed, something would trigger her memory.

Suddenly, I stopped walking, forcing Elizabeth to float right through me, which made me shiver and the fine hairs on my arms prickle.

"What are you doing?" Elizabeth asked in irritation.

She followed my gaze and saw her son, Robert Jr, bundled up in a huge coat, rushing across Main Street ahead of us.

"What's he doing?" I said, but it was really a rhetorical question because I was quite sure Elizabeth had no idea what he was doing either.

The coat he wore was huge, and he was definitely hiding something beneath it.

I held up my hand, waved and called after him, "Robert? Robert Jr, wait up."

He turned and saw me behind him, and his face contorted in a mask of panic, but instead of slowing down, he sped up, racing along Main Street and then ducked down a side street.

Elizabeth was as perplexed as I was. "What on earth is he doing?"

We dashed across the road, trying to keep up with him, but when we finally reached the side street he'd turned down, there was no sign of him.

"He's gone. Why would he be running like that?" I asked Elizabeth.

She shook her head. "I've no idea. It's very unlike him."

"I know he heard me calling him, but he ignored me."

Elizabeth shot me a sideways look. "Well, my son has always been careful about the company he keeps."

My temper flared. "And just what is that supposed to mean?

I'm not good enough company for him, is that what you're saying?"

Elizabeth shrugged. "It's not your fault, Harper. The whole town thinks your family is a little...odd."

I put my hands on my hips and turned to face Elizabeth. "The whole town thinks I'm odd because of things like this. Because I'm trying to help you. And another thing ..." I pointed at Elizabeth, but then slowly dropped my hand to my side when I saw Joe McGrady and Chief Wickham striding along Main Street towards us.

I groaned. Perfect timing. No doubt, in their opinion, I was no longer simply odd. I'd risen to full-blown crazy.

But before they could reach me, Mrs. Townsend called them over. "Cooee, Cooee, Chief Wickham."

Being the polite gentlemen they were, they stopped to talk to Mrs. Townsend. Elizabeth and I took the opportunity to rush off. They would catch up with me before long, and I would have to explain my weird behavior yet again, but I figured I would leave that problem to future Harper.

CHAPTER 15

Jess and I decided to have dinner at the main house with Grandma Grant that evening. Elizabeth's presence could be overbearing, and she'd given me so much to worry about that I'd almost forgotten to be concerned about the mischief Grandma Grant was planning.

We sat at the kitchen table, eating my Grandma's famous potato pie, which was pretty much the only thing she could cook well. Elizabeth had insisted on having a small plateful, and she kept trying to pick up her fork, but her fingers went right through it.

"I thought ghosts could pick things up," she said grumpily. "Poltergeists do it all the time."

I shrugged. "Maybe it just takes some practice."

Grandma Grant looked down at the plate in front of Elizabeth and shook her head. "Honestly, we're pandering to ghosts. Whatever next?"

I quickly changed the subject before Elizabeth got too upset. I told Jess and Grandma what had happened with Archie and the cheese wire, and then told them how we saw Robert Jr running away from us and hiding something beneath his coat.

Grandma Grant put a large forkful of potato and cheese in her mouth and chewed it thoughtfully, then she said, "Well, Robert Jr always was a little bit twitchy."

Elizabeth shot three feet in the air, and I groaned.

"He is not twitchy!" Elizabeth exploded. "He's a good boy, and anyway, you're a fine one to talk. Your son ran off to New York City as soon as he had the chance to get away from you!"

I gasped at Elizabeth's words, and Grandma Grant turned to me with narrowed eyes.

"What did she say?"

"It doesn't matter," I said. "Elizabeth is just a bit upset. I'm sure she didn't mean it."

"I certainly did mean it," Elizabeth said and floated over to Grandma Grant, trying to pinch her arm and failing miserably.

"Elizabeth, please sit down."

But Elizabeth ignored me.

"Harper Grant, tell me what she said otherwise I'm never making you this potato pie again," Grandma Grant said, looking fierce.

I weighed up my options. The pie was certainly the best thing Grandma Grant made, but then again, she was not going to be happy if I told her what Elizabeth said.

I couldn't win.

"Harper, spit it out." Grandma Grant's voice had a steely edge to it.

I blurted out, "Elizabeth said, your son went off to New York City as soon as he got the chance to get away from you."

Grandma Grant put her hands on the table and pushed herself to her feet. Standing up, she pointed to a spot of empty air. "Get out! Elizabeth Naggington, you are no longer welcome in my house. Get out right now!"

"Um, Grandma, she's actually behind you," I said.

Grandma Grant gave a tremendous roar that didn't seem like it could come from such a small lady, and then she started smacking the air behind her, waving her hands around wildly.

Elizabeth screamed as if she was really being attacked, although I was sure she couldn't actually feel Grandma's arms as they passed right through her.

I stood up. "Come on, Elizabeth. You've outstayed your welcome," I said and then looked regretfully down at my half-eaten potato pie.

Trying to help Elizabeth Naggington was turning into a nightmare.

I LEFT Jess trying to calm down Grandma Grant and led Elizabeth back to our little cottage.

I was thoroughly fed up. We hadn't managed to unearth any clues that could help find the killer, and Elizabeth was just getting me into trouble with everybody in town.

"I didn't mean to upset her," Elizabeth wheedled. "But she did insult my son first. So it wasn't my fault really."

I sighed heavily and opened the front door. I just could not be bothered to argue. I didn't have the energy.

I hung up my coat and dumped my purse on the kitchen table and then went through to the bathroom to run myself a bath. I put a large dollop of lavender bubble bath under the taps, and it bubbled up beautifully.

Elizabeth hovered by my side. "Oh, surely you can't still be angry at me."

I turned to Elizabeth with my hands on my hips. "Elizabeth, I'm going to have a bath, and no, you are not going to float through the wall to join me. I need some alone time, just half an hour. That's all I ask."

"Fine," Elizabeth said grumpily.

After Elizabeth finally left me in peace, I stripped off my clothes and slid into my warm, fluffy robe. Then I popped on my huge frog slippers. They were a joke birthday present from Jess, and each slipper resembled a frog's head. Not exactly attractive, but they were surprisingly comfortable.

As the bath was running, I went into the kitchen to make

myself a cup of herbal tea. I looked over the tins of special herbs that Grandma Grant had prepared. I selected the one for relaxation. I certainly needed it today.

I poured the hot water into a mug just as there was a knock at the front door.

My first thought was that Jess had forgotten her key, so I stomped over to the front door in my bathrobe and threw the door open before wandering back to the kitchen.

"That's the second time this month you've forgotten your key," I called over my shoulder.

"Um, I don't have a key," a deep voice said.

I gasped and turned around to see Joe McGrady standing in the doorway.

His eyes slowly traveled down my figure, taking in my fluffy robe before lingering on the odd frog slippers on my feet.

"Nice slippers," he said with a smirk on his lips.

I tightened my robe around me, glaring at him. "I thought you were my sister."

"And I would have thought you'd be a little more careful with a killer running around Abbott Cove."

He shut the door behind him and walked forward until he was standing in front of me.

"Now, Harper, Chief Wickham tells me the Grant family go back a long way, and are an important family in these parts. You need to keep yourself safe. You need to lock your doors, and most of all, you shouldn't invite men into your home scantily dressed, at least, not until we catch the killer."

The sparkle in his eye told me he was joking, but I wasn't in the mood. I was still mad he'd tricked me earlier.

My jaw dropped open. It wasn't as if I had planned on being scantily clad. I didn't have seduction in mind for goodness sake, and if I had, this would hardly be my outfit of choice.

"I was about to take a bath! And it really isn't any of your business what clothes I wear in my own home."

I was overreacting, but something about Joe McGrady just rubbed me up the wrong way. He was way too sure of himself.

"Of course," Joe said. "You're perfectly entitled to wear what-ever interesting footwear you choose. Now, if we can get down to business, you have something to tell me?"

I was thrown for a moment. I didn't know what he was talking about. "What do you mean?"

"I was honest with you yesterday. I told you the murder weapon was cheese wire. And you know someone who uses a lot of cheese wire, don't you, Harper?"

My cheeks flushed red as he moved closer to me, so close, I could see the beginnings of stubble lining his jaw.

I took a step back and folded my arms across my chest, keeping my mouth firmly shut.

"Why didn't you tell me about Archie's cheese wire?" Joe's eyes were no longer sparkling mischievously. He was very serious.

"Archie has the wire because he has a diner, and sometimes he uses it at cheese and wine evenings, but Archie isn't the killer."

"And you know that for sure, do you?"

I nodded. "Of course, I do. I've known him for years. There is no way he killed Elizabeth Naggington."

Elizabeth chose that moment to float between us, which was rather distracting.

"Anyway, instead of focusing on Archie, you should look into Robert Jr. He was acting very suspiciously earlier and hiding something under his coat."

"What?" Elizabeth squealed and flapped her arms up and down in front of my face. "Don't tell him that. You'll get Robert Jr in trouble."

Joe gave me a patronizing look and leaned his weight against the wall. "I can't just interrogate anyone, Harper. I have to have a reason."

"Well, you seem to be interrogating me without a good reason."

A moment passed where we stared angrily at each other, and the tension was only broken when we heard Jess open the front door.

We both turned as my sister entered the room. When she saw us both and noticed I was wearing a robe, her eyes widened, and she put her hands over her mouth. "Oh, dear, I hope I'm not interrupting anything."

Joe gave her a polite nod and then headed for the door. "I was just leaving. Harper, Jess, goodnight."

Jess waited until we'd closed the door behind him before exploding into laughter.

"You look furious," Jess said. "I did interrupt something, didn't I?"

I shook my head. "Only Joe McGrady telling me off."

Jess waggled her eyebrows at me. "That sounds like it could be fun."

"It wasn't," I said grumpily. "He's so arrogant."

Jess cackled with laughter. "Harper and Joe sitting in a tree…" she started to sing.

Even Elizabeth laughed at that. I scowled at them both. "In his dreams."

CHAPTER 16

THE FOLLOWING DAY was my day off from the diner, and although I thought I was probably crazy for even considering it, I decided to use my free time to try and help Elizabeth.

"I think we should go and visit your friend, Victoria," I said.

I didn't mention the fact that Victoria Andrews seemed to be Elizabeth Naggington's only friend in Abbot Cove.

"What a good idea. Poor Victoria. I bet she's missing me terribly. She lives alone, you know. I use to pop round a few times a week, so I imagine she'll be very lonely without my little visits."

Our cottage was close to Grandma Grant's house on the edge of town, but Victoria Andrews lived in the newer residential district, near to where Elizabeth herself had lived.

All of the roads on the development were named after flowers or plants. Victoria lived on Snowdrop Street.

As we walked up the driveway, we could see Victoria inside. She was dressed all in black and standing in the middle of her living room.

"Oh, at last. Someone is showing some respect." Elizabeth smiled happily. "She's wearing black because she is in mourning for me."

I didn't bother to point it out, but Victoria always wore black. I'd never seen her wearing another color. She was on the curvier side, and I think she chose black because it was slimming.

Elizabeth hung back for a moment, gazing in the window and watching Victoria as she dusted the mantelpiece over the fireplace.

"Elizabeth," I hissed. "I'm not spying on people anymore. I'm going to go in and speak to her directly."

Elizabeth shrugged and turned away from the window, following me to the front door happily.

She was in a good mood this morning and had been since I'd told her we would be visiting her friend.

Victoria Andrews wasn't married and didn't have any children. I distantly remembered Grandma Grant telling me she'd been married once, years ago, but had gotten a divorce and moved back to the Cove.

I knocked on the door, and within seconds, Victoria opened it and blinked down at me.

Her sleek, dark hair was carefully arranged in a bobbed style, which reached her jaw line. She didn't hide her surprise at seeing me there.

"Hello, Mrs. Andrews, I wondered if you could spare a few moments for a chat."

Victoria stared down at me, and then looked behind me up and down the road.

When her gaze returned to my face, she said, "You're that Grant girl, aren't you?"

I had a feeling this was all about to go south before I even had the chance to ask any questions.

"That's right," I said smiling at her brightly.

"What on earth would I want to chat to you about? I am rather busy."

I hadn't been expecting this reception. As far as I knew, Grandma Grant had never had a run-in with Victoria Andrews.

"Tell her that you saw her appearance in Abbott Cove's theatrical society last year, and you were so impressed with her performance that you're now considering joining," Elizabeth said as she hovered beside me.

"Um, I saw you in the play last year, and I thought you were ever so good. I wondered if you could give me some tips. I was thinking of joining."

The change in Victoria was magical. She gave me a smile that lit up her face, and she stepped back, gesturing grandly for me to enter her house.

"Why didn't you say so? Come in. We'll have a chat over a nice cup of tea."

Victoria bustled me along into a spacious sitting room full of overstuffed furniture.

"Take a seat. I won't be a minute. I'll just put the kettle on." Victoria gave me another huge smile.

After she'd left us alone in the sitting room, Elizabeth smiled at me smugly. "See, I do come in useful sometimes."

I had to give her that. Sometimes being the operative word.

As Victoria prepared the tea in her kitchen, I wandered around the sitting room, looking at all of Victoria's knickknacks and photographs.

"Oh, look, here's one of me," Elizabeth said and tried to pick up the framed photograph from the mantelpiece. Unfortunately, her hand went right through it.

"Darn it," she said. "I'm never going to get used to that."

"Does it jog any memories?"

"Oh, yes. We went to the fancy restaurant at The Lormont for my last birthday. We invited Victoria as she doesn't get out much, poor thing."

The Lormont was a hotel in the town next to Abbott Cove.

They'd hired a new French chef, and the prices had gone through the roof.

"I meant any memories about who might have killed you."

"Oh," Elizabeth said. "No, nothing like that."

I carried on looking. I picked up a carriage clock and examined it. I wasn't really sure what sort of clue I was looking for.

I scanned the mantelpiece. There was a selection of china animals, another smaller clock, and a wooden pipe. I'd just picked up the pipe to study it when I heard Victoria's footsteps approaching.

Quickly, I shoved it in the back pocket of my jeans and hastily took a seat on the sofa.

I was just in time.

Victoria walked in, carrying a tray. She really had pushed the boat out. She'd made the tea in a proper teapot and had pretty rose decorated china. There was a little bowl of sugar cubes and a pair of silver tongs as well as a plate of cookies.

"I'll be mother," Victoria said as she set about pouring the tea.

"It was such a shame about Elizabeth, wasn't it?"

Victoria looked up and replaced the teapot on the tray. "I thought you wanted to talk about the theatrical society?"

"Oh, I do. I was just very shocked to hear about Elizabeth's passing. I knew you were her friend, and I wanted to offer my condolences."

"Ah," Victoria said. "That's very kind of you. Elizabeth was a very good friend of mine."

I shot a glance at Elizabeth. She was perched on the arm of the sofa, smiling smugly.

I was pleased that at least Elizabeth had had one friend in her life. I'd found that she had rubbed most people the wrong way.

Victoria passed me a cup, and I thanked her and took a sip of my tea.

"What a nice blend," I said politely.

Victoria beamed under my praise. "I get it shipped from England especially. I've always been partial to a cup of tea. I think it's because my great-grandmother was English."

I took another sip of tea and wondered desperately how I could bring up the subject of the murder again without looking crass.

"I don't suppose you know who the police are considering, do you?" I inwardly winced. I'd never been known for my subtlety, so I pushed on. "I can't for the life of me think of anyone who would want to kill Elizabeth."

Victoria's forehead creased in a frown. "Oh, I can think of plenty of people who would, but you didn't come here to talk about Elizabeth, did you? Now, let me see. What advice can I impart? One tip I can give you is channeling your muse."

"My muse?" I had a feeling this conversation was starting to get away from me. If Victoria could think of plenty of people who would have wanted to kill Elizabeth, I needed her to tell me who they were.

But Victoria was lost in thought. "Yes, the best way to get in touch with your inner muse is to go out in the garden — absolutely naked, of course, look up at the sky — it's best to do it on a night with a full moon — close your eyes, empty your mind and give yourself over to the muse."

I tried to control my expression, but it wasn't easy. Even Elizabeth looked a little shocked.

"Well, I suppose everyone has to have a hobby," Elizabeth said.

As Victoria continued to list various methods by which I could get in touch with my muse and improve my acting skills, I began to feel desperate.

This was harder than I'd anticipated. I had assumed that Victoria would be willing to talk about her friend.

"Those tips are very helpful, thank you," I said. "Was Elizabeth part of the theatrical society? Is that how you got to know her?"

"Elizabeth? Oh, no, Elizabeth wasn't very interested in acting. We got to know each other through the Women's Institute and the book club, of course."

Victoria set down her cup of tea and studied me carefully. "Tell me, do you have any acting experience?"

"I did play Mary at a nativity play."

Way to go, Harper. Very impressive.

"And how old were you when you did that?"

"Er, five."

"Well, I suppose all experience counts," Victoria said doubt-fully. "Anything more recent?"

I shook my head. "Unfortunately not, but I'm very eager to learn."

I could tell by the expression on Victoria's face she was not impressed.

So as a last-ditch effort before I got turfed out, I said, "Do you have any idea who could have been responsible for Elizabeth's death?"

Victoria's face hardened. "If I was of a suspicious nature, I would think that you had come here not to talk about the theatrical society, at all, but to try and unearth some gossip about Elizabeth."

I shook my head. "No, that's not the case, at all. I'm only asking because the police came round to question me last night, and it's such a horrible experience for the whole town."

"And you thought you would make a good investigator? Better than the police?"

I shook my head again. "Not exactly..." My voice trailed off as I realized how ridiculous I sounded.

How could I hope to uncover the killer like this? I looked desperately at Elizabeth, hoping she would offer me some help, but she simply shrugged.

Victoria took the half-finished cup of tea from my hand and set it down on the table. "I'm sorry, but I'm very busy. I'm going to have to ask you to leave now, Miss Grant."

Defeated, I slowly got to my feet.

After we were halfway down the driveway, I turned to Elizabeth and hissed, "Well, you weren't much help in there."

"What did you expect me to do? You dug yourself a hole. I don't think investigating is one of your talents, Harper. Your people skills aren't that good, either."

"Thanks very much," I muttered.

We walked in silence away from Snowdrop Street, turning left into Wisteria Avenue, and as we walked along, I suddenly became aware of some very loud music.

It was very unusual for this area. I looked around, surprised to realize the thumping beats were coming from Elizabeth's old house.

I turned to Elizabeth, but she was already floating off towards her old house.

I chased after her, and when I reached her, she was standing beside the sitting room window with her mouth hanging open.

This close to the house, the noise was almost deafening.

There, dressed in tight, pale blue jeans, a black T-shirt, and a cowboy hat, was Elizabeth's husband, Robert, singing along to Bruce Springsteen at the top of his voice and dancing around the living room as he vacuumed.

I understood from Elizabeth's expression that this wasn't a normal afternoon activity for Robert.

We both stood there for a moment, watching. It was like an awful car crash that you couldn't tear your eyes away from.

Eventually, Elizabeth turned to me and said, "He doesn't look like he is missing me very much at all, does he?"

CHAPTER 17

WORK at the diner the following morning passed without much fuss. Having Elizabeth around all the time was really setting my teeth on edge, but thankfully, she had taken to following Loretta around the diner, asking her various questions about ghosts and how they existed.

I imagined Elizabeth had lots of questions. It couldn't be easy for her, and it wouldn't hurt Loretta to do a spot of ghostsitting for me.

Around two thirty, Robert Naggington and Robert Jr came into the diner for a late lunch.

The place was still quite busy, and people walked up to their table to offer condolences. Both Robert Jr and his father wore tragic expressions.

It niggled at me because I had seen Elizabeth's husband dancing around the sitting room to Bruce Springsteen less than twenty-four hours ago. I found it hard to take his grief seriously.

And there was something about Robert Jr that just didn't sit right with me. He looked shifty. I was sure he was hiding something.

Even Archie went over to talk to them. He removed his apron and went and sat in the booth with them for five minutes.

When I went to the table to serve their iced tea, I couldn't help overhearing Archie telling Robert Naggington and his son what a strong lady Elizabeth had been.

It took an effort not to roll my eyes.

I tried to put them out of my mind and get on with serving the other tables, but Elizabeth must had some kind of ghostly sixth sense as she floated through into the main diner, leaving Loretta behind in the storeroom.

"Oh, don't they look sad," Elizabeth said.

"They do now that they're in public," I said sharply. "They didn't look so sad when we saw them yesterday."

Elizabeth pursed her lips. "Grief affects people in different ways, Harper."

"It sure does."

"What's that supposed to mean?"

I shook my head, noticing that a couple of people at nearby tables were looking at me quite strangely.

I started humming, hoping that they would think I'd been

singing to myself. Although, with my singing voice, I wasn't quite sure whether that was worse.

"Oh, excuse me, I would like a refill please."

I turned around and saw Robert Jr waving his empty glass at me.

"I'll be right over," I said and went to get the pitcher of iced tea.

When I walked back over to the table, Robert Jr and his father were deep in conversation with Mrs. Townsend.

"You poor lamb," Mrs. Townsend said to Robert Jr. "You must be missing your mother terribly."

I'd watched enough true crime programs and *Dateline* episodes to know that when a person was murdered, particularly a woman, the killer was usually someone close to home. Someone they knew.

I narrowed my eyes. In my opinion, Robert Naggington and his son were definitely suspects.

After I had poured their iced tea, I asked them how they were doing.

Robert Jr peered at me in a way that very much reminded me of his mother, Elizabeth. He had the same way of looking down his nose at me, even though he was sitting down, and I was standing up. That was obviously a talent he'd inherited from Elizabeth.

"Oh, we are muddling through together," he said.

"I saw you yesterday," I said, watching him closely for his reaction. "You were running away and hiding something under your coat."

Robert Jr visibly paled. His lower lip wobbled.

I knew it! He was showing all the signs of being guilty.

So I pushed on, "What were you hiding under that large coat?"

Then, to my horror, Robert Jr burst into tears.

Not quiet, gentle tears trickling down his cheeks, but huge, great body-wracking sobs.

I stared at him, panicked.

Elizabeth flew over to my side. "What have you done? What did you say to him?"

Mrs. Townsend, who had been sharing the table with the Naggingtons, gave me a very sharp look and said, "Harper Grant, you should be ashamed of yourself. This poor boy has just lost his mother."

There were a few murmurs of agreement from other people in the diner.

I blew out a breath in frustration. It wasn't fair. I was sure he was faking, and I was absolutely positive he had been hiding something.

"He was hiding something," I insisted. "Ask him yourself."

Robert Jr let out an ear-piercing wail.

And at that moment, Archie rushed over. He put his hands on my shoulders and steered me away from the Naggingtons' table. All around the diner, customers were watching me and shooting me daggers.

"I think you should get off home, Harper. We don't need a scene today."

I stared at Archie for a moment, feeling absolutely furious.

I'd believed in him and supported him when he was worried he was about to be accused of murder, and now he was sending me home to avoid a scene with the Naggingtons.

"Fine," I said, shoving my order pad in my apron and undoing the ties around my back.

I hung my apron on the hook by the door, grabbed my coat and purse, and stormed towards the exit.

I'd only been trying to help Elizabeth, but I'd managed to set all the customers in the diner against me.

No doubt this would get back to Joe McGrady, too.

"How could you? I thought you were trying to help me!" Elizabeth snapped at me as I walked past her and headed out the door of the diner.

I left Elizabeth there and stalked home, with the chilly fall breeze swirling around me, feeling absolutely furious.

Jess would still be at work at the library, but I didn't want to talk things through with her yet. She would probably only tell me that it was my fault anyway, which would just annoy me even further.

As I walked down the overgrown path, I could hear rustling sounds ahead. It sounded like the noise was coming from the old greenhouse.

As I got closer, I could see that Grandma Grant was working away inside the greenhouse.

I moved very quietly, taking care over every step I took and wincing when a twig broke beneath my feet.

I wanted to find out what she was up to. She had definitely been acting very suspiciously lately.

When I poked my head round the door, I could see that Grandma was looking down at a little pot on top of the large work bench.

I stepped inside the greenhouse, immediately feeling warmer and sensing the increased humidity in the air. The rich smell of compost and plants surrounded me.

"What are you doing?"

Grandma Grant spun around and put a hand against her chest. "Harper, you shouldn't sneak up on people like that!"

"I wasn't sneaking," I lied. "What have you got there?"

I moved closer so I could see what she was looking at. There was a very small sunflower plant in a pot. I looked at it closely, but I couldn't see anything odd about it.

I looked around the rest of the greenhouse but didn't see anything particularly suspicious.

"I don't know why you're looking at me like that," Grandma

Grant said. "I was just potting up some new plants for Mrs. Townsend."

But as Grandma Grant spoke to me, her eyes kept shifting back to the small sunflower, which was making me feel very uneasy.

"You're back from work early."

I scowled. "Archie sent me home."

"Sent you home? Why? Are you sick?"

I shook my head. "No, it was all because I dared to ask Robert Jr what he was hiding when he ran away from me. I just know he had something under his coat."

"And what did he say?"

"He didn't say anything. He just burst into tears, and everyone thought I was the devil incarnate for upsetting a poor man who'd just lost his mother."

"And Archie sent you home for that?"

"Yes. He didn't stick up for me. Even though I stuck up for him when the police suggested he could be a suspect."

Grandma Grant's gaze shifted down to the sunflower again, then back up to me as she patted my arm. "Things will work out in the end, Harper."

"How? How am I ever going to help Elizabeth pass on when I can't find out who killed her? If she doesn't get peace soon, she'll be hanging around forever like Loretta."

"I thought you liked Loretta?"

"I do. But it's hard enough trying to remember not to respond to one ghost in public, let alone two."

I didn't want to be alone as I knew I would only mope about, feeling sorry for myself, so I spent the rest of the afternoon helping Grandma Grant in the garden.

She had a variety of fall plants that needed to be planted before the frosts came.

It was good, peaceful work, and it calmed me down.

It wasn't until we'd washed up and I was heading back to Grandma Grant's for dinner that I realized I hadn't seen Elizabeth since I'd left her at the diner.

I wondered if she was hanging around and sulking somewhere, and I walked around the outside of the house looking for her.

But there was no sign of Elizabeth. I shrugged, thinking that she'd turn up eventually. She couldn't hold a grudge against me for that long, especially as the only people in the town she could hold a conversation with were Loretta and me.

Jess joined us for dinner. Grandma Grant had prepared a lasagna, and I fixed a salad to accompany it.

The lasagna wasn't terrible by our standards, but it certainly didn't hold its shape. As soon as it was spooned onto the plates, it spread outwards like an oozing mess.

Grandma muttered a few words, clicked her fingers, and the lasagna popped back into shape.

"Grandma!" Jess exclaimed. "You always told us we couldn't use our magic for things like that."

"Do as I say, not as I do," she said smugly.

"That isn't fair," I said.

Grandma shrugged. "Well, I had to set some ground rules when you both moved to Abbott Cove. Besides, Harper, you're only jealous because you can't do spells."

I fought the childish urge to poke my tongue out at her.

We were all sitting around the kitchen table, and it was growing dark outside. I had thought Elizabeth would be back by now.

I was starting to feel anxious. "I wish I knew where Elizabeth had gone."

"She's already a ghost," Grandma Grant said. "It's not like anyone can actually hurt her."

Maybe not, but I was still worried. It wasn't easy transitioning into a ghost, and I hated to think of Elizabeth out there alone.

"I don't even understand why she is angry at me," I said. "I only asked her son the question because I was trying to help her. He was acting so suspiciously."

Grandma Grant swallowed a mouthful of lasagna, and then she said, "Sometimes things aren't what they seem, Harper."

I frowned. It wasn't like Grandma Grant to say something so mystic. "What does that mean?"

Grandma shrugged. "I just thought it sounded good. I read it in a magazine. Lighten up."

I tightened my grip on my fork and used it to spear a lettuce leaf. I opened my mouth to tell Grandma Grant exactly what I thought of her telling me to lighten up when suddenly a warm feeling of calm washed over me.

It didn't matter. None of it mattered…

I was safe here, warm and cozy and…

My head shot up, and I glared at Jess and Grandma. "Stop it."

Both Grandma and Jess tried to look innocent, and Jess said, "Whatever is the matter, Harper?"

I shook my head at them both. I wasn't that naive.

"You're trying to put a calming spell on me." I glared at them, waiting for one of them to deny it, but both of them looked sheepish.

I shook my head. The spell didn't usually work well on other witches, and I was annoyed that I was so susceptible.

I pushed my plate away and stood up.

"I thought you might at least take my concerns seriously," I said. "I'm not some child in need of a calming spell."

Jess raised one perfectly arched eyebrow in response, "Really, Harper, don't overreact."

That was enough to tip me over the edge.

I flung the napkin down on the table and stormed off.

CHAPTER 18

IT'S NOT easy to sleep when you're mad.

I tossed and turned for what felt like hours, before switching on the bedside lamp and plumping up the pillows so I could sit up in bed.

I couldn't believe no one else was willing to consider Robert Jr could be a suspect in his mother's murder. I mean, I understood Elizabeth's reluctance to accept it, but I'd expected everyone else, including the members of my own family, to be more supportive.

Archie, Jess, and Grandma Grant should have at least been willing to hear me out.

I sighed and leaned back against the headboard. I felt bad for upsetting Elizabeth. I probably could have been a little more tactful when I'd questioned her son.

And the fact she seemed to have disappeared into thin air only made me feel worse. She couldn't help being an interfering busybody. I was the only living person who could see and talk to her, so I owed her my help.

Joe McGrady's attitude was even worse. When I told him about Robert Jr hiding something beneath his coat, he'd been dismissive. He was supposed to keep an open mind during investigations, and everyone knew that it was usually the spouse or someone close to the victim, who was responsible. Didn't Joe watch TV?

I should have gone straight to Chief Wickham.

I heard the trash cans rattling outside and got up out of bed to peer out of the window.

It was dark, but I couldn't see anything moving out there. Elizabeth's murder had set me on edge.

I stood by the window for a moment longer just to make sure, aware I was being silly. After all, why would the murderer want to go through my trash? It was probably just a raccoon.

I turned to go back to bed and then suddenly stopped as an idea dawned on me.

It was trash day tomorrow... What if Robert Jr was trying to throw away incriminating evidence?

By the time the police got round to considering him as a suspect, he would have managed to throw away any evidence and the police would never find it.

Maybe that bulky object under his coat had been evidence...

Even if I didn't find whatever he'd been hiding under his coat, I might find something else…maybe cheese wire?

I felt a tingle of excitement. If Joe McGrady wouldn't listen to me, I'd get some evidence myself. That would make everyone sit up and take notice.

I yanked open a drawer and pulled out a black sweater and then selected some black pants from my wardrobe.

I rummaged around for ages looking for a little black hat I used to wear, but I couldn't find it, so in the end, I decided just to tie my hair back and hope for the best.

I took my flashlight from my bedside cabinet. We often had power cuts at the main house and at the cottage. As we were stuck on the edge of town, we suffered from a less than perfect power supply.

I shoved the flashlight in my back pocket and snuck downstairs.

The television was still on in the sitting room. Jess was up late tonight. She never seemed to need much sleep.

I found that suspicious and often wondered whether she'd cast a spell allowing her to get by on less sleep. The idea was appealing as less sleep would mean I could get a lot more done, but I did love my bed.

The television drowned out any sound of my footsteps sneaking out of the house. I closed the front door softly behind me and then set off from the house at a jog.

I soon slowed down. I hadn't run since I was in high school, and after a few hundred meters, I was bent over at the waist, clutching the stitch in my side.

Just because I was going out investigating didn't mean I was some kind of ninja.

I decided to walk the rest of the way, slowly.

On Wisteria Avenue, all the lights were off except one right at the far end. I thought it was Mrs. McCluskey's house. But luckily, the light was far enough away that I was sure no one could see me.

I wandered along the avenue and walked up to Robert Naggington's house as if it was the most natural thing in the world. When I reached the two trashcans at the end of the drive, I paused and looked around.

It was quiet, and I couldn't see any movement anywhere, so I lifted the lid of the trashcan and then recoiled in horror from the smell.

It smelled of rotting fish. My stomach turned, and I started to think perhaps this hadn't been such a good idea.

I lifted my sweater over my mouth, trying to breathe only shallow breaths, which made it a little more bearable. I turned my flashlight on and shined it in the trashcan.

All the trash was enclosed in bags, so I reached in, grimacing as my hand closed around one.

I opened it slowly, pulling a face. In the first bag, I saw the source of the smell. Fishbones, mackerel if I wasn't mistaken.

My stomach rolled rebelliously, and I held my breath as I started to rummage through the bag.

Then suddenly a voice shouted right next to my ear. "What do you think you're doing?"

Elizabeth.

She'd startled me so much, I'd dropped the flashlight in the damn trashcan.

"I'm looking for evidence," I muttered as I tried to fish the flashlight out of the trashcan.

Unbelievable. It had fallen right down to the bottom. How was that even possible?

I leaned down, putting my arm right into the trash and feeling my stomach heave.

"You won't find anything. You're barking up the wrong tree. Robert Jr is a good boy."

"You're his mother. You would say that."

When my fingers finally closed around the flashlight, I pulled it out, and to my disgust, I saw bits of potato peel all over my black sweater.

"Yuk," I said, pulling the peelings off one by one.

I was thankful Elizabeth was okay and still talking to me, even if she was very annoyed.

"Maybe you're right. Maybe Robert Jr isn't involved, but he was definitely hiding something from me the other day, and I want to find out what it was."

"And you think you're going to find it in the trash?" Elizabeth said shaking her head at me.

Well, when she put it like that...

It had seemed a good idea at the time.

I looked reluctantly at the trashcan, but I'd made it this far. There was no point giving up now.

I leaned down determinedly into the trashcan, holding the flashlight in my other hand and pulled something out.

Some kind of wrapper. I read the label. A cheese wrapper, and it still had some cheese in it. Exactly the type of cheese you could use cheese wire for.

I smiled triumphantly and was about to turn and show Elizabeth when I heard footsteps behind us.

I gasped and quickly ducked down behind the trashcans. I'd been so preoccupied with Elizabeth, I hadn't been paying close enough attention to my surroundings.

The footsteps got closer and closer and then finally stopped right next to the trash.

I curled up into a little ball and tried to make myself as small as possible. I wished I was a super witch who could use a spell to make myself invisible.

There was another footstep, and a pair of black boots were now directly in front of me. I stared at them in horror.

Oh no, please, not him. Anybody but him.

"I know you're there. So you may as well come out and stop hiding."

I reluctantly stood up, dusting myself off and trying to look as if this was a perfectly normal situation as I looked up into the sparkling blue eyes of police officer Joe McGrady.

It must have been a trick of the light because I could have sworn I saw a smile twitching at the corner of his mouth.

"Next time you're trying to be stealthy, Harper. You may want to leave the flashlight at home."

"I wasn't trying to be stealthy. If I'd been trying to be stealthy, you'd never have seen me."

Why did I say that? Did I actually want to get myself into more trouble?

Joe cocked an eyebrow at me.

"Now you've blown it," Elizabeth said behind me.

I ignored her. "I'm not doing anything illegal."

"Actually you are."

My cheeks flamed in embarrassment as I pictured myself being carted off to the police station and having to have Grandma Grant come down to bail me out.

The smart thing to do would be to apologize. Of course, I didn't do the smart thing.

"I wouldn't have had to do this if you'd investigated Robert Jr when I asked you to!" I snapped.

Joe looked at me in disbelief and shook his head. "I need a reason, Harper. Law enforcement needs a pesky thing called evidence."

"Aha, then what do you call this?" I proudly held aloft the cheese wrapper I'd found in the trash.

Joe McGrady took a step closer to me and frowned as he looked at the object in my hand. "Is that... a piece of Cheddar?"

I bit down on my lip. It had seemed a lot more convincing a minute ago. Joe looked at me up and down as if I was totally crazy.

I was determined not to let him intimidate me.

"Yes," I said, not allowing him to pour cold water on my theory. I elaborated, "Cheese like this could be cut with cheese wire. Do you see where I'm going with this?" I waggled my eyebrows meaningfully.

Joe didn't reply.

"Don't you see?"

Joe frowned and looked at me as if I was indeed off my rocker, as Grandma Grant would say.

"No, Harper. I don't see."

He pointed at the wrapper in my hand. "Go and put that trash back, and I'll take you home. We'll talk about this in the morning."

I shrugged. I suppose it could have been worse. At least he wasn't taking me to the police station.

Reluctantly I put the cheese wrapper back in the trash and retied the trash bags, grimacing at the smell.

"I'm glad I don't have to work trash collection," I said. "It really stinks."

"You don't smell so hot yourself," Joe McGrady said.

My jaw dropped open in shock. "That wasn't a very gentlemanly thing to say!"

"I never claimed to be a gentleman, Harper," he said and gave me a wink, making me blush again, but this time for a different reason.

Elizabeth chuckled beside me. She was enjoying this far too much.

CHAPTER 19

"WELL, are you going to tell me what you did last night?"

My spoon hovered over my cereal as I'd been just about to take a bite.

I dropped the spoon back into my bowl, splashing the milk.

"Last night? What makes you think anything happened last night?" I said.

I knew I was acting suspiciously. I'd never been good at evading the truth, especially when it came to Jess's questions. She was unusually perceptive.

Jess said nothing. She simply tilted her head to the side and gave me a look. I hated that look.

"Fine," I said grumpily.

I knew it was futile trying to hide it from her. No doubt Joe would have told Chief Wickham, who would have told his wife, which meant it would be all over Abbott Cove by lunchtime, and Jess would find out anyway.

I shrugged. "It's nothing really. No big deal. I just went out last night to do a little bit of investigating, and Joe McGrady caught me."

Jess's eyes widened. "A little bit of investigating! Harper, what did you do? If Chief Wickham finds out you've been interfering in his investigation, especially when it's the only murder we've had in the town since records began, he's going to be furious."

"Thanks for that," I said, deadpan.

I could always rely on Jess to make me feel better. Not.

"I wasn't exactly interfering anyway," I said. "I figured since no one believed that Robert Jr was hiding something, I'd look for a little evidence myself. It's not like I broke into their house. I just went through the trash."

Jess balked. "You went through their trash? Yuk."

"Yes, it wasn't the most pleasant experience. And then Joe found me elbow deep in fish bones. It wasn't my finest hour."

"And you're upset because you think Joe won't like you anymore?"

"What? No, of course not. I don't give two figs about what Joe thinks of me."

Jess gave me a knowing look and grinned. "Of course you don't, Harper."

I glared at her as I took a mouthful of cereal.

"Did you find any evidence?" Jess asked.

"No, of course, she didn't. The very idea that Robert Jr could be involved in my murder is just ridiculous," Elizabeth said, appearing out of nowhere.

"He was definitely hiding something." I turned and looked at the spot where Elizabeth was hovering over my shoulder. "I just wanted to find out what it was."

Jess looked through Elizabeth. "I take it Elizabeth is back?"

I nodded glumly, although I was pleased she was back and safe.

"Yes, I am here. So you can stop talking about me behind my back."

I sighed. "Jess isn't talking about you behind your back, Elizabeth. She wants to help just as much as I do."

Jess pulled a face.

"Well, you're investigations last night didn't get very far, so what are we going to do now?" Elizabeth asked.

Good question. I had no idea what to do next.

I guessed the main thing I had to deal with this morning was Joe. I'd worried all night about what he would tell Chief Wickham.

He told me we would discuss it in the morning, so I was expecting a phone call at any moment to send me to my doom.

After we'd finished breakfast and I was washing dishes, Grandma Grant burst into the cottage.

"Harper!" She yelled, and I cringed.

I guessed she'd heard what I'd gotten up to last night.

I wiped my hands on a towel and walked slowly out of the kitchen like someone condemned to meet her fate.

Grandma Grant was staring at me as if I was the most irritating person in the world. She looked mad, but not head-exploding mad, which was good.

I put two and two together and guessed that she hadn't yet heard from Joe McGrady or Chief Wickham.

"Do you two not answer your phones? Archie has been trying to get hold of you, Harper. He's called me twice already this morning."

I frowned. "I'm not supposed to go back to work until this afternoon. My shift doesn't start until two."

"I don't know about that. I just know Archie is trying to get hold of you, and I'm not your personal answering service."

"Okay," I said, holding up my hands in surrender. When dealing with Grandma Grant, it was easier to go along with her most of the time.

I went into my bedroom and picked up my cell phone. I'd forgotten I'd put it on silent last night. It was a new phone, and for some reason, it pinged every time I got a new notification. Every time I got an email, it woke me up.

I dialed Archie's number, and he answered the phone after a couple of rings.

"Harper, can you get down here now?"

I could hear the normal bustling sounds of the diner in the background.

"Yes," I said, "But my shift doesn't start until this afternoon, does it?"

"I know, but I need you to come in, and — Oh no, that's all I need. Tommy Breton is back, and he's bound to make his usual awful mess. I'd better go. See you soon," Archie said, and then he hung up.

I stared down at the phone. No apologies for sending me home early in disgrace yesterday, I thought huffily.

Only a second later, the phone rang again. It was Archie again. "Sorry, I forgot to say Chief Wickham is here, and he wants to talk to you."

Before I could ask Archie to elaborate, he'd hung up again.

I bit my lip, feeling sick as I imagined Chief Wickham tearing strips off me.

But then again, if the chief wanted to see me at the diner and not the station, maybe he wasn't going to tell me off.

Perhaps Chief Wickham wasn't annoyed I'd been investigating on my own. Maybe he thought my suspicions were correct.

I smiled, carried away by my daydream, imagining the chief

putting Joe McGrady in his place and making Archie apologize for not believing me.

I combed my hair, put on my coat and then set out towards the diner with Elizabeth hovering by my side.

As we walked, I turned to her and said, "I'm glad you've forgiven me, and you can see that I'm only trying to help you."

Elizabeth gave me a sideways look. "I'm still not happy with you, Harper. But as no one else can see me, I don't really have much choice."

Charming.

CHAPTER 20

WHEN I ARRIVED at the diner, Robert Jr, Joe McGrady and Chief Wickham were sitting in a booth.

I swallowed hard. That didn't quite fit in with my daydreams. I had a strong feeling I wasn't going to be getting any pats on the back. I was far more likely to be in for a stern ticking off.

I hesitated beside the coat hooks and watched them. They hadn't yet noticed I'd arrived. Joe and the chief sat on one side of the table facing Robert Jr, who was fiddling with the salt shaker nervously. He pushed back his shirt sleeves.

Joe leaned his large frame back in the seat. He looked brawny compared to Robert Jr, who despite his generous girth, had unusually thin, spindly arms.

The chief had an empty plate in front of him, and he shifted back to loosen his belt slightly. Both Joe and Chief Wickham were studying Robert Jr closely and listening to Robert talk.

I couldn't hear their conversation from where I stood, and I couldn't hide there all day. I needed to get it over with. I took a deep breath and hung up my coat and purse.

Then I saw Archie bustling out of the kitchen, holding two plates stacked with pancakes.

He nodded in the chief's direction, letting me know in no uncertain terms he wanted to see me.

I chewed on a thumbnail nervously, and then when I realized I had fallen back into the habit of biting my nails, something I hadn't done since I was a teenager, I shoved my hands in my pockets and walked towards them.

The chief was the first to see me. "Ah, Harper, I heard there was a little bit of a scene here in the diner yesterday?"

I took a shaky breath and nodded, bracing myself for a telling off. I cringed, waiting for Chief Wickham to mention the trash last night, but instead he gestured for me to sit down next to Robert Jr.

I did so nervously and caught Joe McGrady's eye.

He didn't look angry. He even smiled at me a little reassuringly.

"It's okay, Harper," Joe said. "We've found out what was behind Robert Jr's suspicious behavior."

"You have?" I turned to Robert in surprise.

Robert Jr was looking even paler than usual. He had a cup of untouched coffee in front of him, and he kept wringing his hands.

"I didn't kill her. I could never do that. I loved my mother."

I sensed Elizabeth moving behind me, but I didn't dare turn around.

I glanced back at Chief Wickham and Joe to see if they believed Robert Jr because he sure looked twitchy to me.

"But you were right, Harper. I was hiding something," Robert Jr said, his voice trembling.

Aha, I knew it!

Joe nodded encouragingly at Robert Jr, so he would finish his story.

"When you saw me the other day, I'd taken a couple of mother's antique vases to sell to Maurice Flanagan."

I frowned. Why was he trying to hide that? Surely, he would have inherited some of Elizabeth's belongings anyway.

"So why were you hiding them under your coat?"

Chief Wickham supplied the answer as Robert Jr's lower lip began to wobble, and he looked like he was in danger of bursting into tears yet again.

"Robert has a gambling debt. The vases in question were particularly valuable, and he sold them for quite a bit less than their market value to get some ready cash."

"I'm so ashamed," Robert sobbed beside me.

Finally, I dared to turn around and look at Elizabeth.

Who knew it was possible for a ghost to turn even paler? Elizabeth's face was white.

* * *

I LEFT Chief Wickham and Joe to deal with Robert Jr, as Elizabeth hovered in the corner of the diner, trying to process this new information. Learning her precious son was addicted to gambling had hit her hard.

I went to see Archie before I left, to tell him I'd see him for the afternoon shift.

"I'm sorry for sending you home like that yesterday, Harper," Archie said, tucking his order pad into his apron and ringing up a bill on the till. "I just thought it was the best way to stop everyone flying off the handle."

I shrugged and smiled. "It's okay. You were in a difficult position. I see that now."

When Sarah hollered out another order, Archie quickly rushed off, and I headed out of the diner.

I decided to call on my sister at the library. She'd get mad if I didn't update her on the latest developments and she had to hear it from the town's gossips.

Jess waved at me as soon as I walked in. There was a small group of kindergarten children in the children's section making quite a racket. "I thought libraries were supposed to be quiet places."

Jess rolled her eyes. "Try telling that to a class full of kids under five."

She gestured for me to come behind the counter as she stacked books onto a small wheeled trolley. "So, what did Archie want? Did he apologize?"

I nodded and filled Jess in on what had happened at the diner, telling her all about Robert Jr's gambling addiction.

"So you were right about one thing," Jess said. "He was hiding something."

"Yes, but it doesn't look like he's the killer so I'm back to the drawing board."

I picked up the top book on the stack — a book on cross-stitch. Why couldn't I have a nice normal life and a hobby like that?

I sighed and put down the book. I wouldn't have time for anything like that while I was so busy trying to help Elizabeth.

"Is Elizabeth with you?" Jess said and looked around the library as if she would be able to see her.

I shook my head. "I left her at the diner with Loretta. She's taking the news that Robert Jr was addicted to gambling quite hard. Loretta will never admit it, but she's enjoying having another ghost around even if it is Elizabeth Naggington."

"What are you talking about?" I looked down and saw one of the small children had left the group and was now standing directly behind me.

"Er... nothing. Just grown up talk."

149

The little girl wore her hair in plaits and stared up at me with an earnest expression. "You were talking about ghosts."

I looked at Jess, desperate for help.

She clasped the little girl's hand and led her back to the group of children sitting cross-legged on the floor.

The stress was making me careless. The last thing I needed was the town to find out I could see and talk to ghosts.

When Jess returned, she looked thoughtful. "So you don't have any new suspects?"

I shook my head miserably. "Not even one, and I don't have the first idea where to start. It's looking more and more like Elizabeth Naggington could be here to stay."

Jess reached out and patted my hand. "It's early days, Harper. Chief Wickham and Joe McGrady will find out who did it, eventually. They must have left some evidence. There's no such thing as a perfect crime. Maybe you should just leave it to the experts."

I nodded. Jess was probably right. This whole business had caused me nothing but trouble since I'd started. Maybe I was better off supporting Elizabeth but leaving the investigating to the experts.

"Have you got the rest of the day off?" Jess asked.

I shook my head. "My shift starts at lunchtime, but I'm free for the rest of the morning."

Jess smiled. "Good. Can you go and keep an eye on Grandma Grant? She was acting ever so strangely earlier when she came in here asking to look at my new spell book."

I frowned. That was all I needed at the moment — Grandma Grant adding complications.

"What do you think she's up to this time?"

"No idea," Jess said. "But knowing Grandma Grant, it's going to be pretty spectacular."

I left Jess and headed up the hill to Grandma Grant's house. I caught the leg of my jeans on some brambles poking out from the shrubs along the overgrown trail.

We'd been nagging Grandma Grant to let us clear this section of path for ages. It was almost surrounded by a thicket, various plants twisted and wound themselves into a thick, green mass, like something out of a fairytale. But Grandma Grant said she liked it how it was. She said it stopped people wandering onto her property.

Halfway along the path, Elizabeth caught up with me, hovering slowly and looking very disappointed.

I felt bad for her. She'd built Robert Jr up in her mind to be the perfect son, and this had come as quite a blow.

"Now that Robert Jr's problem is out in the open, he'll be able to get some help," I said. "Maybe this is a good thing."

"A good thing?" Elizabeth looked at me incredulously. "Sometimes you say the strangest things, Harper."

I was about to reply when suddenly I heard a large crack followed by a scream.

That sounded like Grandma Grant!

I took off at a run, jumping over tree roots and puddles until I burst into the opening. Panting for breath, I stared in horror at the greenhouse.

Outside, Grandma Grant's cat, Athena, stood staring up at the sky. Her black hair on the back of her neck bristled as she meowed loudly.

I looked up.

A huge sunflower had broken through the roof and was now towering over the house.

And it was still growing…

I looked around desperately for Grandma Grant. "Grandma? Where are you?"

"Oh, my goodness," Elizabeth said as she arrived by my side and looked up in disbelief at the huge sunflower towering above us. "Is it still growing? How is that even possible?"

I knew exactly how it was possible. Grandma Grant had cast a growing spell, and it had gone badly wrong.

I knew all about bad spells. I was quite an expert at them. That's why I avoided them as much as I could.

I needed Jess, but it would take her too long to get here.

"Grandma!" I called again, heading towards the greenhouse, taking care not to tread on the splintered glass.

"In here, Harper, quick!" Grandma Grant's voice came from inside the greenhouse.

I quickly burst in, imagining her caught beneath the stalk, or trapped somehow.

But when I saw her, I exhaled in relief. She was unhurt.

Bustling from side to side, she frantically flicked through different spell books. At the same time, she grabbed things off the shelves.

Her gray hair, which was normally tightly held in a bun, was flying all over the place.

"What have you done?" I asked.

"There's no time to explain," Grandma said. "I need your help now. I have to cast a quick reversal spell. I need..." Grandma Grant hesitated as she squinted at the list of ingredients in the spell book.

Some spells required a potion to go along with them, and I guessed a reversal spell was one of them.

"Now let me see. I've got rosemary and thyme, and I've got some dried juniper berries around here somewhere. Two cat's hairs, that's easy enough. So I just need..." She turned to me. "I need pondweed and a pebble from the bottom of the pond. Can you get that for me?"

I would much rather have been tasked with getting the rosemary or the thyme than a pebble from the bottom of the pond.

"Really? But it's all slimy at the bottom of the pond."

"Harper, this is not the time to argue with me." She pointed in the direction of the pond. "Chop chop."

My shoulders slumped as I stomped outside, but I quickened my pace when I turned and saw the sunflower was almost at the level with the roof of Grandma Grant's huge old house.

I sprinted the final few steps to the pond and then hesitated as I looked at it reluctantly.

The surface was smooth, and a couple of dragonflies skirted over the top. Unusual to see them so late in the season, but then again they were the least of my concerns right now.

I got down on my hands and knees beside the pond and plunged my arm into the cold water. I inhaled sharply as my fingers slipped on the bottom and groped about in the mud and slippery green stuff that lived down there.

I pulled a face as my hand closed around a stone and lifted it up. My arm was covered with pondweed.

I rushed back to Grandma Grant, and she held out a pot for me. "Good girl. Put it in there, Harper."

I did as I was told and then stood back and watched as Grandma Grant mixed the ingredients together. She muttered a few lines as she sprinkled the potion over the bottom of the sunflower stalk.

When she finished, I heaved a sigh in relief.

"Oh, thank goodness, that's over." I noticed with amazement that the sunflower began to shrink a little.

I had expected it to stop growing but hadn't realized it would shrink back to its normal size. I would have to renew my efforts to learn more about casting potions and spells. They were extremely useful.

I was about to congratulate Grandma Grant on her spell-casting skills when I remembered I was supposed to be angry with her for creating the problem in the first place.

"Grandma, look at the state of your greenhouse. It's going to take a fortune to repair all this. You really should stop using your spells experimentally."

Grandma Grant looked at me and raised an eyebrow. "With potions and spells, a witch should constantly be learning. Even a witch of my age," she said, pointedly.

"Well, I suppose I'd better help you clear up. We don't want anyone getting cut on all this glass."

"Actually, Harper, we may have a more pressing matter to attend to."

I raised an eyebrow and looked at Grandma Grant suspiciously. "What now?"

Grandma Grant shifted her gaze. I turned and saw row after row of tiny seedlings on the bench next to us.

My gaze flickered down to them, and then I gasped. "You didn't? Tell me you didn't use a potion on all of these plants?"

Grandma Grant shrugged. "Well, it seemed to be working quite well on the first sunflower plant. How was I supposed to know it would keep on growing?"

"Quick! Put the reversal potion on them. Fix them before they start to grow."

I'm afraid I need a new potion for every single plant.

My eyes widened. No, she couldn't be serious.

"And you know what that means, don't you, Harper?"

I groaned. I knew exactly what that meant. I was going to have to go back to the pond and get more pebbles. A lot more pebbles.

By the time we finally finished, I was exhausted. I pulled off a strand of pondweed from my sweater, flicked back my wet hair and looked angrily at Grandma Grant.

"I can't believe you did all this in secret. If you'd told us, at least we could have been prepared."

"Don't be ridiculous, Harper. If I'd told you, you would have stopped me."

Grandma Grant walked back to the house with Athena at her heels, leaving me speechless behind her.

CHAPTER 21

FEELING FRAZZLED, I got back to the cottage and hung up my coat. Thanks to Grandma Grant and her uncontrollably growing plants, I was running late. I had things to do today, starting with laundry.

As I headed to the laundry basket in my bedroom, Elizabeth zoomed in circles around me.

"That was exciting! That was the most interesting thing that's happened to me since I've been a ghost."

"I'm glad it was so entertaining for you," I said as I gathered up my laundry and started carrying it out of the bedroom.

But Elizabeth didn't respond to my sarcasm. Instead, she pointed to the floor. "What's that?"

Something had fallen from the pile of clothes in my arms. I

knelt down and dumped the clothes on the floor, and reached for it.

"Oh, I'd forgotten about that. It's a pipe."

"I know it's a pipe," Elizabeth said impatiently. "But what on earth are you doing with my husband's pipe?"

I turned the pipe over in my hands and studied it. It was the one I'd picked up from the mantelpiece at Victoria Andrews' house. I'd quickly put it in my pocket to hide it when Victoria had returned with the tea, and I'd forgotten to return it.

Elizabeth was staring down at the pipe. "It was his favorite. He must have missed it."

"Are you sure it was Robert's pipe? One pipe looks much the same as another to me."

Elizabeth nodded. "Of course, I'm sure. Look, there's a little chip in the wood there. I got him another one for his birthday a couple of years ago, but he wouldn't give this one up. He said it just didn't feel the same."

I held the pipe next to the window, to get the best light, and studied the little chip. Elizabeth was right.

I tried to suppress the feeling of dread rushing through me. "Elizabeth, I found this pipe at Victoria's house."

Elizabeth frowned, opened her mouth, and then abruptly shut it again.

We stood staring at each other for a moment, and then Elizabeth gritted her teeth, clenched her fists and whirled around, half gliding and half flouncing out of the cottage.

"Wait! Elizabeth, wait!" I grabbed my coat, and still clutching the pipe, I followed Elizabeth.

"I'll give that harlot a piece of my mind," Elizabeth fumed as she hovered along the path towards the center of town. "She pretended to be my friend."

Between trying to calm Elizabeth, and suggesting there could be another perfectly logical reason for Victoria having the pipe, I fumbled for my cell phone.

"What logical reason, Harper?" Elizabeth demanded.

"Er…"

Elizabeth was right. I couldn't think of a reason why Victoria had the pipe, other than Robert had left it there, which meant… Oh, dear, I didn't want to think what it meant.

My fingers felt thick and clumsy as I dialed the police station's number.

"The simplest explanation is often the right one," Elizabeth said in a cold voice.

"Do you really believe they were having an affair? Maybe it was just an innocent visit, and Robert left his pipe behind."

"Innocent? Pah!" Elizabeth sped up, and I struggled to keep up with her.

If Robert had been having an affair, that was certainly a motive for him to get rid of his wife.

When the phone was answered, I burst out, "Chief Wickham?"

"Yes."

"This is Harper Grant. Could you have a word with Victoria Andrews about Elizabeth's murder? The thing is, I think Robert may have been having an affair with Victoria."

Chief Wickham was silent for a moment on the other end of the line, and then he sighed heavily.

"Harper, you really should have learned your lesson. You can't just accuse people of things like that without any evidence."

Elizabeth was pulling away from me, so I quickened my strides, and breathlessly tried to persuade the chief to go and talk to Elizabeth. I started telling him about the pipe.

"Now, Harper, Joe told me about the trash incident outside Robert Naggington's house. You've really got a bee in your bonnet about this. You need to stop interfering and leave it to the professionals."

Damn, Joe McGrady. Did he really have to tell Chief Wickham about the trash thing? I thought I'd gotten away with it.

"I'm quite prepared to leave it to the professionals," I said. "That's why I'm asking you to go and talk to Victoria."

Chief Wickham sighed heavily again. "I'm busy at the moment, Harper. There's been a dispute out on Main Street over parking. Betty Turnbull and Brenda Burke. Again. They've been at it hammer and tongs for the last half an hour, and somehow, I've got to try and stop them from killing each other. On top of this, I have to investigate Elizabeth's murder by the book. That means following procedure and questioning people in an approved fashion. Not running over to question people when you ask me to."

"But..."

"Look, I will talk to Victoria later today, but you have to promise to leave this to the police. Don't go around to see Victoria yourself. Promise me that, Harper."

I hesitated for a moment. Elizabeth was still traveling full steam ahead.

"Sorry, Chief, You're breaking up," I said, and then hung up and ran after Elizabeth.

I finally managed to catch her just before she reached Victoria's house.

I watched in horror as Elizabeth leaned down, picked up a large decorative stone from the flower bed in Victoria's front garden and threw it at Victoria's window.

CHAPTER 22

My eyes widened as I stared at Elizabeth in shock and a small amount of admiration. She'd finally managed to harness the power to move objects. She turned into a poltergeist. Obviously, her anger had helped.

"Elizabeth," I hissed. "Stop it, immediately. I'll get the blame for that."

Victoria appeared at the door. Her usually impeccable bobbed hairstyle was slightly messed up. She stared at her broken window and then back at me.

"What on earth do you think you're doing?"

Before I could answer, Robert Naggington appeared just behind Victoria's shoulder.

His shirt was unbuttoned.

Elizabeth screamed in anger, but of course, nobody heard it but me.

I pulled the pipe out of my pocket and held it aloft so they could both see it. "This gave you both away. Have you told the police about your little affair?"

Robert began to hastily button his shirt, and he and Victoria exchanged guarded glances.

"I think you'd better come in," Victoria said.

Okay, so it probably wasn't the smartest move to go inside when I strongly suspected Robert had killed his wife, but I did anyway.

Victoria smoothed down her hair and led me into the sitting room. "Please take a seat, Harper."

She was acting very strangely, almost as if I'd just popped by for a social call.

"Can I get you something to drink? A cup of tea? Or perhaps lemonade? It's homemade."

Thrown slightly, I blinked and then shook my head. "I'm fine, but I would like an explanation."

"Well, I for one could do with a drink," Robert said, raking his hand through his hair.

"I'll get you one, Robert. I won't be long," Victoria said. "Then we'll explain, Harper. I'm sure you think badly of us right now, but hopefully, you'll understand when you hear our side of the story."

Victoria walked out of the sitting room, but I still didn't sit down.

I stared at Robert Naggington and said, "Did your wife know about your affair? Did you decide to get rid of her, so you and Victoria could be together?"

Elizabeth was circling Robert, trying to smack his head, which was a little distracting.

It seemed, even though she'd managed to lift a rock outside, she wasn't able to physically hurt Robert, which was probably a good thing.

Robert looked horrified. "What? No, I would never have hurt Elizabeth. You've got it all wrong."

I frowned. He did look genuinely shocked at my accusation, but maybe he was just a very good actor.

I was completely out of my depth and started to wish I'd waited for the police. Was I about to make a complete fool of myself again by accusing the wrong person?

I looked to Elizabeth for help, but she was absolutely of no use. She was now trying to pummel Robert into submission, but he just stood there oblivious.

I heard footsteps, and Victoria came back into the room, holding a tray with three glasses of lemonade. She put the tray on a low coffee table, picked up a glass and handed it to me.

"Please, Harper, sit down and let us explain."

Reluctantly, I did as she asked.

Then Robert spoke up, "Victoria, darling, would you mind making tea instead? The lemonade is lovely, but the sugar plays havoc with my bad tooth."

"Of course, darling," Victoria leaned down to stroke Robert's cheek, and Elizabeth looked like she might explode.

Victoria left Robert and me alone in the sitting room and went to get tea. I was feeling distinctly uneasy. Could this very ordinary man be a killer?

Robert sat opposite me on a flowery print armchair with his elbows on his knees, and his head bowed forward.

"It wasn't me. I would never have hurt Elizabeth. I admit I was a weak man, and I succumbed to temptation."

He looked up at me, pleading with his eyes for me to understand. "You know what Elizabeth could be like. She was a rather determined person, and Victoria was much more of a free spirit and very kind."

I sat there, looking sternly at Robert Naggington, and didn't reply. I wasn't sure what he expected me to say. Just because Elizabeth could be difficult at times and rather domineering, it didn't give him an excuse to cheat on her.

I took a sip of lemonade as I considered what he'd said.

If he'd been a good man, he would have stood up to her, and they could have overcome their difficulties or separated. But this sneaking around behind her back was a horrible thing to do.

"Harper, you know what Elizabeth was like. You'd seen her in the diner in one of her moods. Surely you can understand that I needed a little escape."

I shook my head. To be honest, it was becoming increasingly hard to concentrate on what Robert was saying because, at that moment, Elizabeth was pummeling his head with her fists. Robert paid absolutely no heed to her attack, but it was still distracting.

"No, Robert, I'm afraid I don't understand. Elizabeth was not —" Elizabeth stopped pummeling and gave me a sharp look. I needed to choose my words carefully. "I mean, Elizabeth could be difficult to get along with, but that didn't give you the right to cheat on her."

Robert's shoulders slumped, and his gaze fell to the floor. "You're right of course. I wished I had talked to her more. Maybe we could have sorted things out. We were very much in love once."

Elizabeth moved a small distance away from Robert, so she could look down on him. She had stopped trying to hit him around the head. I supposed that was progress.

"I knew it," Elizabeth said. "That hussy! It was all Victoria's fault. Now, let's see what I can destroy of hers," Elizabeth said, moving towards a large, expensive-looking, blue and white vase on the sideboard.

"No!" Too late, I realized I'd spoken aloud and tried to cover my outburst with a pretend cough.

"Are you okay, Harper?" Robert asked, looking concerned. "Have some more lemonade."

I took a large gulp and shot daggers at Elizabeth. "I'm fine now, thank you."

"I'm a weak man, Harper. I took the easy way out. Victoria was welcoming and kind, but I never loved her like I loved Elizabeth."

Unfortunately, Robert chose to say those words just as Victoria was returning with the tea tray. Her eyes widened in shock, and the tea tray fell from her hands, clattering to the floor.

The porcelain smashed, and the brown tea and milk spilled all over the Persian rug.

CHAPTER 23

ROBERT TURNED IN HORROR, and when he realized Victoria had overheard him, he said, "Victoria! Wait. That didn't come out right. I didn't mean it."

He chased Victoria out of the room as she ran out sobbing.

"He always was a weak man," Elizabeth said as she hovered beside the couch.

I sighed and stood up. "I think we had better go and leave them to it. We've caused enough havoc for one day, and Chief Wickham is going to be furious with me when he finds out I came here after he asked me not to."

My head was pounding, and I felt strangely dizzy. This whole experience had been incredibly stressful. Yet again, I'd focused on the wrong suspect.

Robert was certainly guilty of cheating on his wife, but I was pretty sure he hadn't killed her.

"It looks like it is back to the drawing board again," I said to Elizabeth, or at least, that's what I tried to say, but somehow my words came out all slurred and mixed up.

Elizabeth frowned and looked at me with concern. "Are you okay, Harper?"

My mouth tasted all furry, and the dizziness was getting worse. "I think I better get home, Elizabeth. I'm not feeling too good."

I reached down to pick up my purse, and when I straightened back up, my head swam. I saw a strange vision in front of me. I blinked a couple of times not quite believing it. Was I hallucinating now?

In front of me, Victoria stood in the doorway. She smiled coldly, and in one hand she was holding cheese wire.

I looked down at my half-finished glass of lemonade at the same time as Elizabeth.

"You can't go yet, Harper," Victoria said in a dangerously calm voice. "You haven't finished your lemonade."

"Don't drink it! I think she's drugged it," Elizabeth shouted.

She was right. I wobbled a little, feeling very unsteady on my feet.

Why had I come here when the chief told me not to?

I found myself wishing I'd paid more attention to Jess when

she talked about her spells. I could really do with a "get the heck out of here spell" right now.

Victoria chuckled.

"I almost thought you had it," she said as I tried to keep myself upright by leaning on the back of a chair. "When you showed me the pipe, I thought the game was up, but you have no idea, do you?"

I took a step back, trying to get as far away from Victoria as possible. I shook my head. "Why? Why did you kill Elizabeth? Did you really kill your best friend just to be with Robert?"

Victoria gave me a slow clap. "Well done. You got there eventually. The trouble is I don't think you're going to be able to prove it, are you?"

Robert gave a horrified gasp. "Victoria, what are you saying?"

"I did it for us, snookums, so we could be together."

Elizabeth pulled a face. "Yuk. Snookums? I think I just threw up a little."

I looked at Victoria and then Robert in turn. The room was spinning. What had she put in that lemonade?

"Did you know about this?" I asked Robert.

Robert shook his head vigorously. "I had no idea. Victoria has always been such a sweet lady. I never lived up to Elizabeth's expectations, and Victoria accepted me for who I was... I can't believe she would have hurt Elizabeth. She's such a gentle soul."

Victoria chose that moment to make a run for it.

I couldn't let her get away without being punished, so I chased her through the sitting room and into the kitchen.

It wasn't the wisest choice.

To my horror, I realized getting me in the kitchen had been her plan all along.

She wasn't going to run.

She was about to commit another murder.

Mine.

She brandished the cheese wire in front of her and took a menacing step towards me.

"No! Wait! I told the police I was coming here, and they know everything. You won't get away with this."

"I think I'll take my chances. Robert will back me up. We'll say that it was you who killed Elizabeth—everyone in Abbott Cove knows you're a weirdo anyway. You and that odd family of yours are an accident waiting to happen."

That did it. I snapped.

I wasn't about to let her insult my family like that, and there was no point just standing there waiting for her to attack me with the cheese wire. I had to catch her off guard.

I charged straight at her, intending to knock her to the floor, but she was stronger than I'd expected, and as she braced herself against the refrigerator, she slipped the cheese wire over my head.

Robert entered the kitchen and screamed, "No! For goodness sake, Victoria, stop!"

"Get off her, you mental old bag," Elizabeth growled.

Somehow Elizabeth managed to pick up a heavy pot from the stove and throw it at Victoria's head.

The pot hit its target with a clunk, and it was enough to make Victoria loosen her grip on the cheese wire, and I managed to break free and I fell to the floor.

Then, seemingly out of nowhere, I felt a pair of strong hands tuck under my arms and lift me to my feet.

Chief Wickham's large face loomed over me. His gray hair was sticking up on end, and his ruddy cheeks were redder than usual.

"Are you okay, Harper?" the chief asked.

Joe McGrady was snapping a pair of handcuffs on Victoria as Robert began to cry.

"Would it really have killed you to wait, Harper?" Joe asked. "You could have been hurt."

I grinned at Chief Wickham and then Joe before turning to Elizabeth. "Thank you. You saved my life."

"We wouldn't have had to if you did what you were told," Joe grumbled, thinking I was talking to him.

"You interfering witch," Victoria screamed at me, and I flinched at her choice of words.

Chief Wickham took over from Joe. "Victoria Andrews, you are under arrest for the murder of Elizabeth Naggington."

As the chief maneuvered Victoria outside. Keith, the temporary officer, who always got the worst jobs, tried to console Robert.

"Are you okay, Harper?" Joe McGrady asked.

I nodded, although I was feeling decidedly dizzy still. "I think Victoria may have put something in my drink. I feel a bit wobbly."

I stumbled as I spoke, and Joe reached out to steady me. He crooked a finger beneath my chin and tilted my head up so he could look into my eyes.

He really was incredibly good-looking. I grinned up at him stupidly.

"We'll get Doc Morrison to take a look at you, but I might have to take you to the hospital."

I smiled dreamily. Things had certainly worked out. We'd found Elizabeth's killer, and best of all, Joe wasn't angry with me.

I watched Keith Tucker hold Robert Naggington back as Chief Wickham deposited Victoria in the back of the police cruiser. He looked like he could quite cheerfully have killed Victoria.

"Silly man." Elizabeth was watching him, shaking her head sadly. She floated over to the police car.

"You were a hero," I said grinning up at Joe.

Joe frowned. "I think we'd better get you checked out pretty soon."

"You have lovely eyes. Did anyone ever tell you that?"

Joe grinned. He tried hard not to, but in the end, he couldn't help himself. "Are you flirting with me, Harper Grant?"

"No!"

But I continued to grin at him. "Unless you would like me to?"

Joe McGrady stared down at me for a moment. His gorgeous blue eyes studied me closely. Then he leaned down until his lips were next to my cheek. I could feel his breath against my hair as he whispered, "Maybe when you're not under the influence of narcotics, Harper."

I sighed and sat down on the grass beside Victoria's driveway, and I waited for Doc Morrison to come and check me out.

Joe held up a finger. "Stay there, Harper."

I gave him a fake salute. "Yes, sir."

I looked over at Elizabeth, feeling glad we had finally managed to nail her killer, but at the same time sad she'd found out all those secrets about her family along the way.

Goodness knows life was certainly simpler without a man around. But as my gaze magnetically found its way back to Joe McGrady, I grinned. Life might be simpler without them, but it was far more interesting with them.

CHAPTER 24

JOE DROVE me to the hospital. I didn't remember much of the drive as I fell asleep almost immediately after I buckled my seatbelt.

The next thing I knew, I was in the city hospital, and a doctor was shining a light in my eyes.

He fired a range of quick questions at me, what day of the week is it? Who is the president? And so on.

When he was finally satisfied, he flicked off his flashlight and smiled. "I don't think you'll have any permanent damage. You're very lucky as you ingested a large dose of tranquilizers. We've administered the antidote, which appears to be working now, but we are going to keep you in for a few hours to make sure."

"Thank you, doctor," I said.

I was relieved I would be okay, even if I did have to stay in the hospital longer than I would have liked.

I couldn't wait to get home. I turned to look at Joe, who was sitting on the chair beside my bed. He'd stayed with me since we'd arrived at the hospital, other than a couple of minutes he'd taken to pop outside and call Grandma Grant, letting her know what was happening.

"It's good of you to keep me company, Joe, but you don't have to stick around. I'm sure you've got better things you could be doing."

"I'm staying right here," he said and gave me a dazzling smile.

Just when I almost thought he cared, he added, "You'll only do something else crazy if I leave you alone, and I'm sworn to protect the citizens of Abbott Cove."

I pulled a face and hit him on the arm. "Jerk."

"I can see you're starting to feel better, Harper."

As Joe checked through the messages on his cell phone, I snuck a glance at him. The way his hair fell over his forehead made me want to reach out and push it back. He was a nice guy really, even if he didn't want me to think so.

He might think I was crazy, but he had taken me to the hospital, and he was still sitting at my side.

I thought the drugs were slowly wearing off as I was starting to feel more self-conscious. I realized I was wearing a hospital gown, and I really hoped that Joe wasn't sitting next to me when the nurses had removed my clothes. I couldn't remember.

I chewed my lip. I hoped I hadn't snored in the car, or even worse, drooled!

"What's up, Harper?" Joe reached out and put a hand on my arm. "You're looking worried about something."

I shook my head. "I'm not worried. I'm fine. I was trying to think of a way to say thank you. If you hadn't been there, Victoria would have killed me, too."

I liked the feeling of his warm hand on my arm.

"It's my job, Harper."

"Protect and serve."

He nodded. "That's right."

I smiled as a feeling of warm contentment passed over me. "Well, you were very good at your job." I peered over the edge of the bed to see if he still had the handcuffs. "You were quite an expert with those handcuffs," I said. "Very impressive."

"Are you flirting with me again, Harper?" Joe's face was serious, but his blue eyes sparkled mischievously.

I snatched my arm away. "Goodness no!"

"That's a shame."

I felt butterflies in my stomach, but the effects of the drugs were fading, and I was starting to feel mortified by the things I'd said over the past few hours.

Still, if you didn't try…I swallowed hard and then said, "Well, if you wanted to… Maybe we could…"

But I was saved from embarrassing myself further when I heard Grandma Grant's piercing voice say, "This infernal place is like a rabbit warren. How is anyone supposed to find the patient they are looking for? We are never going to find her. Harper!"

I looked at Joe and winced.

Joe chuckled. "It sounds like you have some other visitors."

He stood up, squeezed my hand and said, "I'll go and get them and then leave you to it. I can swing by later if you need a lift home?"

I shook my head. "That's kind of you, but I'm sure Jess will give me a lift home, thanks."

Joe nodded once and gave me a brief smile before stepping out of the cubicle to go in search of my family.

I leaned back against the pillows.

Maybe I could ask Joe out. After all, I was a modern woman. Before I could think about it anymore, Grandma Grant burst in. "Oh, Harper, you would not believe the trouble we had finding you."

Ignoring Grandma Grant's grumbling, Jess flew over to the side of my bed and hugged me tightly. "Harper, don't you ever do that again! Chief Wickham told us you confronted Victoria alone even though you thought she might be the killer."

"It was quite clever of you," Grandma Grant said, grudgingly. "I wouldn't have expected you to be quite so intuitive."

It was on the tip of my tongue to confess that actually I hadn't realized Victoria was the killer until it was almost too late, but instead, I decided to bask in Grandma Grant's admiration. She didn't hand out compliments easily, and I was going to take them while I could get them.

Jess pushed my bangs back from my face. "I've spoken to the doctor, and he said if he is happy with your blood test results, which should be back in the next hour or so, we can take you home."

"Tonight?"

Jess nodded, and I sighed with relief. I couldn't wait to get home and back to normal.

Grandma Grant perched on the side of my bed and complained about the lumpy mattress, which actually wasn't lumpy at all.

Jess leaned forward and whispered, "Is Elizabeth around?"

I shook my head. "I haven't seen her since Joe put me in his car to bring me to the hospital."

"Do you think she's passed on?"

"I hope so."

And I really did. Despite all our differences, I really wanted Elizabeth Naggington to now find peace.

CHAPTER 25

WHEN MY BLOOD test results came back fine, Jess and Grandma Grant were allowed to take me home.

Jess brought me a pile of books from the library and tucked me up on the sofa with a blanket. She also brought me what looked like a year's supply of chocolate. Well, it was probably a year's supply for a normal person, but eating chocolate was a special talent of mine, and it would probably only take me a few days to eat it.

For supper, Grandma Grant made me her special chicken soup. She told me it was an old family recipe, so I half-expected to see a few eyeballs rolling around in it, but luckily it only appeared to be made from chicken, stock and a few vegetables.

I took the bowl from her and tried to look grateful. I took a tentative sip and was surprised to realize it wasn't actually that bad. It tasted pretty good.

I suspected magic, but I didn't ask. Sometimes, it was better not to know, especially with Grandma Grant.

After I'd eaten my soup and Grandma Grant had returned to her own house, Jess and I sat in the sitting room. I curled up on the sofa, and she sat in the armchair, both of us reading books.

I was reading a particularly soppy romance and imagining myself and Joe McGrady as the main characters when suddenly I saw a movement in the corner of the room. When I looked up, I saw Elizabeth.

She hadn't moved on.

At first, Elizabeth didn't speak. She drifted over and sat down on the edge of the sofa. She'd learned how to do that now without falling through the seat.

"Are you okay?" she asked.

"I'm fine."

Jess looked up from her book. "Is Elizabeth back?"

I nodded, and Jess grimaced. We'd both been expecting Elizabeth to have moved on.

"Nothing's happened," Elizabeth said. "I don't understand it. We found out who the killer was. So I should be moving on, shouldn't I? I don't have any other unresolved business."

I searched for the right words to reassure her. I wanted to

make her feel better. "I imagine it does take a little while, Elizabeth. It's probably not an instantaneous process."

But Elizabeth's face was still sad as she said, "Just in case I do go soon, I wanted to thank you, Harper. I know I can be a little prickly at times."

At times? She wasn't kidding.

"But I am grateful to you for your help. I'm going back to my house now. I know Robert Jr can't see me, but I want to say goodbye in my own way."

I nodded. "Of course, I understand."

After Elizabeth had left, I read for a little longer until I'd finished the book and then leaned back on the sofa to daydream.

I didn't see any reason why I couldn't ask Joe McGrady out on a date. What was the worst that could happen? He could only say no.

I cringed under my patchwork quilt as I imagined him saying no. Perhaps I wouldn't ask him straightaway. There was no rush.

The following day, Grandma Grant announced she was taking us to the diner for a celebratory meal.

Archie enveloped me in a warm hug as soon as I walked through the door.

"I'm so glad you're okay, Harper. It's all around Abbott Cove how you foiled the killer single-handedly. You're so brave!"

"Well, actually it wasn't really single-handedly. Deputy McGrady and Chief Wickham played quite an important part."

"Yes," Archie said, waving my words away. "But they're trained to do that, you're not. And you faced up to a killer all on your own. You're amazingly brave."

As soon as we walked through the diner and went to sit in a booth, I realized that Archie was right. It was all around the town.

People kept coming up to our table and congratulating me for my incredible investigative skills. I started to feel more and more guilty. It was really Joe and the chief who should be getting the credit. They'd saved the day, after all, and it wasn't as if I'd actually identified Victoria as the killer until after she'd drugged me.

When our meals came out, I saw that Sarah had piled my plate with extra sweet potato fries. Everyone was so sweet and concerned, and it reminded me why I loved living in Abbott Cove.

Everybody liked to stick their noses into each other's business, but the community pulled together, and it really was a lovely place to live.

Mrs. Townsend was next to wander up to our table. "I'm so glad you're okay, Harper." Mrs. Townsend turned to Grandma Grant. "You must be ever so proud of your granddaughter."

Grandma Grant gave a shrug. "She gets it from me."

After Mrs. Townsend had left our table, Grandma Grant

turned to me and said grudgingly, "You're not a bad witch, I suppose. You really should learn more about spells, though."

"Er… I would have thought you'd be more grateful. I was the one who called out the glazier to repair the greenhouse after your spell went wrong and the mutant sunflower grew through the roof."

"That's my point exactly, Harper. If you were better at spells, you could have helped me and gotten the plants back to normal faster."

"I did help you. I got those horrible, slimy pebbles out of the bottom of the pond."

"Well, anyone could have done that," Grandma Grant said, dismissively.

Jess realized I was looking at Grandma Grant as if I would like to murder her, so she laid a calming hand on my shoulder.

"Let it go," she whispered.

I was incredibly annoyed. I'd spoken to the glazier and managed to skirt around all his awkward questions about how on earth we managed to get such a hole in the roof of the greenhouse.

Loretta passed through the diner, inspecting everybody's meals and then floated up to my side.

"I know you can't reply right now, Harper, but if you can excuse yourself for a minute, Elizabeth is waiting just outside. She wants to talk to you."

I smiled and nodded, but didn't respond out loud to Loretta.

I excused myself from the table and headed outside.

The fall air was clear, crisp and fresh, and I saw Elizabeth standing beside the antique shop, two doors down. Loretta floated out of the diner and followed me.

When Elizabeth saw me approaching, she looked up and smiled.

"I wanted to say thank you again and... Goodbye. It's time for me to go. I can't explain...it's just a feeling. Would you keep an eye on Robert Jr for me?"

I hesitated and looked back towards the diner. Robert Jr was currently installed in a corner booth, getting slowly drunk.

"I'll do my best," I promised.

I took a step back as Elizabeth's whole body started to shimmer.

It was beautiful, like the facets of a crystal. Different colors, sparkling and merging into one and rising upwards slowly until she disappeared.

I felt tears in my eyes as I turned to Loretta. "That was beautiful."

Loretta looked tired as she stared at the empty spot where Elizabeth had been. "Yes, it was. I wonder if it will ever happen to me?"

There had to be something in Loretta's past holding her back, some unfinished business, but it really wasn't the sort of question I felt I could ask her.

I figured if she wanted me to know, she would tell me eventually, and maybe one day, she could pass on peacefully, too.

We walked back together and stepped into the diner. As the warm air and smells of cooking wrapped around me, I looked over and saw Grandma Grant scolding Jess for not finishing her vegetables.

I grinned. I really was very lucky. I had a family that loved me, and I lived in a beautiful town. What more could a girl ask for?

Maybe a date with Joe McGrady.

Maybe one day. For the moment, I was very happy with the way things were. Life in Abbott Cove was good.

FIRST CHAPTER OF A WITCHY MYSTERY

"Have you seen this, Harper?" My sister, Jess, breathlessly rushed through the diner, before stopping in front of the table I was clearing and waving a brightly colored flyer in front of my face.

I plucked it from her fingertips and read:

The Yoga Goddess invites you to her new studio. The first lesson is free so what are you waiting for? Be prepared to get in touch with your inner goddess…

I pulled a face.

"There's a class tomorrow morning. I've signed us up," Jess announced proudly.

"I don't know," I said doubtfully as I scooped up two empty coffee cups. "I'm not sure I even have an inner goddess."

Jess pouted. "Come on, Harper. It will be fun."

The idea of turning my body into a human pretzel didn't sound like fun to me. It was all right for Jess. She was flexible.

My sister had inherited all the sporty genes. I'd inherited the genes that made me suited to sitting on the couch and reading books.

Jess loved trying out different types of exercise. She had been over the moon when a Pilates class started up in Abbott Cove last year. Unfortunately, Mrs. Tomlinson, who was eighty-three, had taken to the machines a little too enthusiastically. She'd snuck in the night before her class, intending to get a little practice, and ended up tangled in the machine, hanging upside down. She screamed for help until she was rescued by the fire service. The Pilates instructor had left Abbott Cove shortly afterward.

As Grandma Grant said, no one could accuse the residents of Abbott Cove of being unenthusiastic. Sometimes, they were a little too enthusiastic for their own good.

I caught sight of my boss, Archie waving at me frantically. We were a little short-staffed today.

I agreed to go with Jess just so I could get back to work before Archie popped a blood vessel. I mean, it was only yoga. How bad could it be? I should suggest the class to Archie. It was meant to be relaxing, and Archie could use a little relaxation. I liked my boss, but he was highly-strung. He referred to himself as a perfectionist, but I saw him more like a walking advert for high-blood pressure.

"I'll go, but I don't think the woman running the classes is going to be very popular."

"Why ever not?" Jess asked.

"She has been in the diner a few times, and she is..." I searched for the right word but came up blank. "Difficult."

Difficult wasn't a strong enough word to describe Yvonne, in my opinion, but work wasn't a suitable place to say the other word that popped into my mind.

Jess frowned. "I think you have already made up your mind not to enjoy the class."

I rolled my eyes. "Wait until you meet her then you'll know what I mean. Are you staying for coffee?"

Jess shook her head. "I can't. I have to open the library. It's just me this morning."

I finished clearing the table as my sister left the diner as swiftly as she'd arrived.

My hands piled high with a stack of plates, I turned and walked straight through Loretta. I shivered.

"Well, that was rude," she said, folding her arms over her chest.

"Sorry, I muttered. I didn't see you there." I kept my voice down. The last thing I wanted was for the people in the diner to think I was talking to thin air.

I should probably explain in case you think I'm a nutcase. My name is Harper Grant, and I'm a witch. My particular talent is seeing ghosts and communicating with them. It's actually my only talent.

I come from a long line of witches and warlocks. My sister Jess is a whiz at spells. She works at the library and is more of a traditional witch than me. My Grandmother, Grandma Grant, is very powerful, which can be quite dangerous, as I'm convinced she has lost her marbles. It's nothing to do with her advancing years, though. She's always been a little crazy.

My father turned his back on magic, so Grandma Grant was delighted when Jess and I wanted to explore our magical abilities. She was overjoyed when she realized I was a "communicator," apparently communicating with ghosts is a rare ability. Unfortunately, she wasn't so impressed with my other magic skills, which are practically non-existent.

Loretta, through whom I had just walked, is the diner's resident ghost. She had haunted the diner for years as far as I can tell, long before I started working here. A few months ago, I tried to ask her when she'd become a ghost, but she'd looked horrified and informed me it wasn't polite to ask a lady her age. That hadn't been exactly what I meant, but I let it slide.

Loretta looked slightly mollified at my apology, but before she could reply, the diner door opened, and three women entered.

"Speak of the devil," Loretta muttered.

I didn't need to ask to whom she was referring.

It was Yvonne Dean, the self-proclaimed Yoga goddess. She

had visited the diner every day since her arrival in town. Although, I had no idea why. She never ate anything.

I took the plates through to the kitchen and then hurried over to get them settled.

Old Bob, who was sitting at his normal table, almost choked on his bacon as Yvonne waltzed past his table. She seemed to have that effect on men. Tall, blonde, glamorous and extremely thin, she demanded their attention.

I was glad Archie was in the kitchen. I didn't want to see him fawning over her again. It was embarrassing.

The three women sat at one of the tables by the window. Yvonne wore a pair of oversized sunglasses, which covered half her face, and she had a yellow, patterned, silk scarf tied around her neck. On her left, sat her sister, Carol. She had a chin-length bob of mousy-brown hair. Every time I'd seen her, I'd thought she looked like she was about to burst into tears. On Yvonne's right, sat her PA. I'd forgotten the woman's name, but I recognized her from their previous visits. She wore her dark hair pulled back in a tight bun, and her expression was sour, almost a scowl.

"What can I get you today, ladies?" I asked, taking my order pad from my apron.

Yvonne took off her dark glasses and peered up at me. "Why don't you remember my order? I've been in here every day for a week, and I've had black coffee on every occasion."

"Of course, I remember," I said, forcing myself to smile and keep my tone pleasant. "I thought you might be tempted by one of our specials. I can recommend the pancakes, and the lemon muffins are fresh out of the oven."

"Oh, lemon muffins are my favorite," Carol said, brightening up and looking decidedly less tearful.

Yvonne's head snapped up. "A moment on the lips, a lifetime on the hips, Carol."

Carol was stunned into silence.

An uncomfortable pause followed her comment, although Yvonne didn't seem to notice.

"We'll just have three black coffees, please," Carol murmured eventually as she stared miserably down at the table.

"I'll have a lemon muffin," the PA said with a tight smile, and I could tell she wanted to have one to show Yvonne she couldn't boss her around.

Carol put a hand to her mouth to smother a gasp, as though she couldn't believe anyone would have the audacity to go against her sister's wishes.

Yvonne raised an eyebrow but said nothing.

I grinned at the PA, thinking good for you. I was tempted to have one myself.

I headed over to the coffee maker and poured three cups. As I prepared to bring the ladies their coffee, I noticed Archie peering out of the kitchen hatch.

His cheeks were flushed, and his eyes were wide as he craned his neck, trying to see the table where the three women were seated.

"Archie, what on earth are you doing?"

"Is that Yvonne?"

I nodded. Archie came over all embarrassed and had giggled like a schoolgirl every time Yvonne had visited the diner, but he'd never hidden in the kitchen before.

I rolled my eyes. "Why don't you come out and say hello?"

Archie shook his head. "I can't. I've got bacon grease splattered all over my shirt."

"I'm sure she won't mind a little bacon grease on her number one fan," I teased.

Archie's cheeks grew redder, but he shook his head again. "I couldn't possibly. What would she think of me?"

Loretta, who was hovering just behind my shoulder, made a sound of disgust and said, "Men! I can tell you one thing, Harper. Men haven't changed much from my day. They always get taken in by a pretty face."

I left Archie fretting in the kitchen. Sarah, our usual cook, was away for a couple of days, visiting her mother in Rhode Island, so Archie had taken over all the kitchen duties.

I selected a particularly large, deliciously fluffy lemon muffin from the display counter and added it to the tray. As I was carrying it over to the table, Chief Wickham and Deputy Joe McGrady stepped inside the diner.

I shot them a quick smile and told them to take a seat while I served the ladies their coffee.

"Is there anything else I can get you?" I asked.

Yvonne smiled slowly as she looked over my head. I knew she was looking at Deputy McGrady, and who could blame her.

He was nice to look at. I couldn't deny it. He was tall, handsome and a little too cocky for his own good.

"Perhaps you could introduce us to these two handsome gentlemen," Yvonne said in a low, seductive voice.

I couldn't help noticing her change in tone from earlier when she had snapped at me for not remembering her order.

I only just managed to stop myself rolling my eyes. I smiled through gritted teeth and turned to introduce Chief Wickham and Joe McGrady.

"This is Yvonne Dean, Abbott Cove's very own Yoga Goddess," I said, thinking how silly it was to claim to be a goddess.

Whatever faults Yvonne had, a lack of self-confidence wasn't one of them.

Both men seem to be so enamored with Yvonne's cool blonde, good looks they didn't comment on the fact I'd introduced her as a yoga goddess.

I started to introduce the other two women and realized in horror, I still couldn't remember the name of Yvonne's assistant. I was usually good with names.

"This is Carol, Yvonne's sister, and—"

Before I could finish, Yvonne interrupted, "Thank you. That's all for now. We'll call you when we need you."

"I..." My voice trailed away. Was she really dismissing me? I hadn't even taken Chief Wickham and Joe's orders yet. I was starting to understand how Carol felt.

"I'm Louise," Yvonne's assistant said, but no one appeared to notice.

Her comment barely registered with me because I was watching in horror as Yvonne stood up and began to flirt with both the chief and Joe.

Worse still, both men seem to relish her attention.

"You're fighting a losing battle there, Harper," Loretta whispered in my ear.

I shrugged. It really wasn't any business of mine.

Finally, the chief managed to turn his attention away from Yvonne. "Harper, just the person I needed to see."

I smiled. They may have ignored me at first, but at least, the chief was talking to me now. It was nice to know I wasn't invisible.

I shot a triumphant smile at Yvonne, but she was too busy giggling at something Joe had said to notice.

I soon wished the chief had continued to ignore me, though.

"I need to have a word with you about your grandmother," the chief said.

I closed my eyes and groaned. "What has she done now?"

"She's been lying in front of the mayor's car again."

That wasn't good. My grandmother's favorite means of protesting anything she didn't like or approve of was to lie down in the road, disrupting traffic. Luckily, Abbott Cove was only a small town, and traffic was light. I had no idea what the bee in her bonnet was this time.

"I suppose she has a good reason for protesting," I began. "Is she out there now?"

I reached around my back, ready to untie my apron and try to persuade Grandma Grant to see reason.

The Chief shook his head. "No, I've no doubt she would have stayed there all day, but the Mayor's chauffeur managed to drive around her, and I guess she realized lying in the road after that was pretty pointless. But you really need to stop her doing things like this, Harper. Not only because it disrupts the town's traffic, but because it's dangerous. She could get hurt."

I nodded. "I know. I'll have a word with her," I said, even though I knew it wouldn't do any good. Grandma Grant was a law unto herself, and she never listened to my sister or me.

"Wait… Since when did the Mayor have a chauffeur?"

The chief shrugged. "He hired Old Bob's nephew, Graham, a month ago."

I opened my mouth to respond but then arched an eyebrow as I saw Joe McGrady slip into the same booth as Yvonne, Carol and Yvonne's assistant.

"Do join us, Chief Wickham. It's a bit of a squeeze, but I'm sure you won't mind getting cozy," Yvonne said with a saccharine sweet smile.

I wanted to throw up. Instead, I smiled brightly and asked the chief and Joe what I could get them.

"Well," the chief said, rubbing his belly. "I have already eaten breakfast, but that muffin looks delicious," he said eyeing the lemon muffin I'd brought over for Yvonne's assistant.

"They haven't long been out of the oven. They are still warm," I said.

The chief smiled broadly. "Go on, you've twisted my arm. I'll have a lemon muffin and one of those fancy coffees you make with the frothy milk."

"Coming right up," I said and then turned to Joe. "Deputy McGrady?"

Joe looked at me, and a puzzled smile tugged at his lips. He was probably wondering why I was being so formal and not just calling him Joe.

I intended to show Yvonne by example that our law enforcement officers in Abbott Cove should be treated with respect, but it wasn't working out too well.

I stood there awkwardly as Yvonne fondled Joe's bicep.

"Oh, I can see you take exercise very seriously. You should try my yoga class. We could do with some more men to balance things out."

I was gratified to see Joe shift in his seat, so Yvonne's hands fell from his arm. "Yoga is not really my thing."

"You never know until you give it a try," Yvonne said in a seductive purr.

I cleared my throat trying to get his attention again.

When that didn't work, I lost my patience.

"What can I get you?" I snapped, feeling irritable.

Joe looked up, "Uh, sorry, Harper. I'll have the same as the chief. One of those lemon muffins, but I'll take my coffee black."

"Coming right up," I said, turned around, and for the second time that day, I walked straight through Loretta.

* * *

I spent the next half an hour, wiping down tables that were already clean, and topping up sugar bowls that were already full, all the while, keeping my eyes firmly on Joe, Yvonne and the chief, who all seemed to be getting along like a house on fire. The same couldn't be said for Louise and Carol. Both women sat quietly, seemingly content to let Yvonne be the center of attention. I imagine Yvonne wouldn't have stood for anything less.

Poor Carol had watched Louise, Chief Wickham and Joe polish off their lemon muffins. I was tempted to bring another one to the table and tell Carol it was my treat, but it really wasn't any of my business. If she wanted to be bossed around by her sister, there wasn't much I could do about it. But I hated to see anyone pushed around like that, and Carol looked very miserable.

After I'd finished cleaning table seven, I walked back over to the booth by the window and decided to give Carol another chance to order a muffin.

"Can I get you guys anything else? Are you sure you won't change your mind about that muffin, Carol?"

Carol hesitated, but then she shook her head and looked down miserably at her lap.

The Chief had eaten his muffin in three bites. "You should have one. They are absolutely delicious," he said and then turned his gaze on Yvonne. "Why don't you have one, too? You look like you could do with a treat."

The saccharine smile left Yvonne's face, and she pursed her lips. "I can assure you I am quite sweet enough. Anyway," she said as she turned her head and pointedly gazed at my hips. "Some of us watch our figures."

I felt my cheeks heat up. That was a low blow. I had put on a few pounds over winter. What can I say? I work at a diner where the food is delicious, and Sarah makes the most amazing carrot cake.

But I wasn't Carol, and I wasn't going to let Yvonne make me feel guilty.

I completely ignored Yvonne and turned again to Carol. "Are you sure, Carol? I could put one in a bag for you to take out."

Carol looked up. Her eyes flickered to her sister and then back to me before she gave a tentative smile. "Yes, I'd like that. I'll have one to take out."

I smiled to myself as I walked back to the counter to bag up a muffin for Carol.

It was only a small step, but I was glad she'd stood up for herself.

Shortly afterward, Old Bob left his corner table followed by the chief and Joe McGrady.

The three women remained in the booth, having a deep discussion. I only caught every other sentence or so, but it sounded like they were talking about setting up the new yoga business.

I imagined Yvonne must be doing very well for herself to employ a personal assistant and her sister to help. It surprised me that she was setting up a base in a town as small as Abbott Cove. We weren't exactly a bustling metropolis, and I wasn't quite sure how many customers she would have.

But I suppose Yoga paid well. She had a very expensive-looking watch on her wrist, not that I knew much about that sort of thing, and her clothes looked expensive. I was pretty sure she had a top of the range Coach purse on the floor beside her feet.

It had been quiet so far this morning, and it didn't appear to be getting any busier as we approached lunchtime. Sometimes the diner could be like that. Other days, we'd have busloads of tourists descend upon us, and we'd be packed out. We never knew what days we were going to be busy, but as Archie said, at least it kept us on our toes.

Archie still hadn't dared to come out of the kitchen, which I found amusing and irritating at the same time.

I began to fold some napkins — one of those jobs I tended to do when it was quiet — when all of a sudden I heard Yvonne raise her voice.

"Oh, for goodness sake. Do I have to think of everything? Can you never think for yourself? I suppose this is another mess you expect me to get us out of."

I looked up but quickly looked down again as Yvonne caught me watching and scowled.

I didn't mean to eavesdrop, but if she spoke so loudly in a public place, I would hardly classify that as eavesdropping.

Yvonne huffed out an impatient breath and shrugged on her jacket. "Well, why are you just sitting there? Go and pay the bill," Yvonne snapped at her sister.

Carol hastily got to her feet and rushed over to me.

"Can I get the check?" she mumbled miserably, rummaging through her purse.

"Of course, I would have brought it over to you," I said as I started to ring their order up on the till.

"I thought I'd better come over to the counter. Yvonne is in rather a hurry."

After Carol had paid the check, the three women left the diner.

I stared after them, and a strange sense of unease made me shiver.

Loretta drifted in front of me, and as the door closed behind them, she said, "That woman is going to cause trouble for Abbott Cove, mark my words."

I exhaled a long breath. I had a horrible feeling Loretta was right.

A NOTE FROM DANICA BRITTON

Thank you for reading my Harper Grant Series. I hope you enjoyed this book! If you have the time to leave a review, I would be very grateful.

If you would like to be one of the first to find out when my next book is available, you can sign up for my new release email here: Newsletter

For readers who like to read series books in order here is the order of the series so far: 1) A Witchy Business 2) A Witchy Mystery 3) A Witchy Christmas 4) A Witchy Valentine 5) Harper Grant and the Poisoned Pumpkin Pie 6) A Witchy Bakeoff.

http://www.dsbutlerbooks.com/danicabritton/

f

ALSO BY DANICA BRITTON

Harper Grant Cozy Mysteries

A Witchy Business

A Witchy Mystery

A Witchy Christmas

A Witchy Valentine

Harper Grant and the Poisoned Pumpkin Pie

ACKNOWLEDGMENTS

To Nanci, my editor, thanks for always managing to squeeze me in when I finally finish my books!

My thanks, too, to all the people who read the story and gave helpful suggestions.

And last but not least, my thanks to you for reading this book. I hope you enjoyed it.

Made in the USA
Las Vegas, NV
17 June 2022

50385451R00125